Marshal of Storytown

Storytown regarded Marshal Gene Cardinal as the best lawman they'd ever had. Hadn't he tamed the wild miners, taken control of the streets and re-imposed law and order when all his predecessors had failed to do so?

But everything changed forever the day the marshal's former lover came to town. She was followed closely by Colt champion Ash Quentin, her most recent rejected conquest, who had vowed to win her back or kill her.

Overnight Storytown became a battlefield and sixgun law would rule again until either the gunfighter or the marshal were dead.

By the same author

Where Tillerman Rides

Marshal of Storytown

Clint Ryker

A Black Horse Western

ROBERT HALE · LONDON

© Clint Ryker 2006
First published in Great Britain 2006

ISBN-10: 0-7090-8202-9
ISBN-13: 978-0-7090-8202-6

Robert Hale Limited
Clerkenwell House
Clerkenwell Green
London EC1R 0HT

Typeset by
Derek Doyle & Associates, Shaw Heath
Printed and bound in Great Britain by
Antony Rowe Limited, Wiltshire

CHAPTER 1

I AM THE LAW

Quietly Marshal Cardinal drew the Colt .45 from its holster on his right hip.

Tincup lay silent and moon-stricken all about the Storytown marshal's vantage point, high in the blackness of the old barn. Yet he knew he'd heard something, was aware of a tingling of the nerve ends that stemmed as much from a sharp awareness of the breed of man he was hunting here as from his certainty that some alien force was abroad in the deep night.

His gaze focused on the lamplit windows of the Paiute Saloon halfway along the block. Back in Storytown where Gene Cardinal and his deputies imposed law and order over ten thousand citizens and countless trouble spots, he knew every saloon, gambling hall and low dive like the back of his hand. He wished he knew the Paiute, for instinct

5

and observation warned him that the man he'd ridden twenty miles from Storytown to find might be holed up there. But as he didn't know the layout, he would wait. He was no way certain that he could outshoot Billy Cheeko if it should come to that, but was solid sure he could out-wait the hardcase. He could wait as long as it took.

The slender young outlaw lolling against the Paiute's rough bar had little talent for waiting, as evidenced by the way he kept flipping a silver coin and glancing toward the batwings.

The hellion who'd hightailed from Storytown after shooting an innocent citizen, had no inkling the renowned 'Mr Marshal' was anyplace near. As far as Cheeko was concerned he'd covered his tracks with his usual skill and was now concentrating exclusively on another serious matter entirely.

The men he expected to show up here tonight were three former partners who'd recently joined him in an attempted stage stick-up in which Cheeko had lost his temper, winged a driver and cost a fourth partner his life.

Tincup was the dead partner's home town. They'd been boasting they would square accounts with him, had proclaimed it far and wide. But how scared did Cheeko look, sipping whiskey and flipping that silver coin?

Not scared at all, if the saloonkeeper was any judge. And that worried the man plenty. For he knew Cheeko a little and knew the former quartet all too well. He could smell big trouble on the night air.

'Say, Billy boy,' he said at length, 'would you like to wait outside? I mean, I jest got the the porch painted, and it took me nigh three months to replace this here bar mirror after the last time it was busted. . . .'

He fell silent, the color suddenly draining from his sunken cheeks.

The sound of thudding hoofbeats wafting in off the prairie seemed to strike the ear like a beaten drum, rhythmical, menacing.

'Freeze, swamper!' Cheeko breathed as the man made to duck low. He wagged a cautionary finger as his right hand reached for his gun handle. 'Normal and natural. That's how it's got to look, pard. *Compre?*'

Three riders galloped into town. They made a swift turning around the ornamental fountain then reined in sharply, noisily demanding to know if 'trigger-happy' Cheeko happened to be in town.

The Paiute was accustomed to trouble. Men melted from sight; sounds were swallowed up; a piano tinkled away into silence.

'We know you're here, Cheeko, you bum! Better get out from under her skirts and take your medicine like a man – you trigger-happy son of a bitch!'

The trio was liquored up and loaded for bear.

Cheeko knew that was how they would be, which was why he was no longer anyplace near the Paiute. Swifter than a shadow, he was already abroad on the moonshadowed streets someplace, and even the highly alert Storytown marshal started when the indistinct and shadowy figure appeared silently in an alleymouth on the far side of the riders. Cheeko's voice was soft in the deepening quiet.

'Right here, lads!'

The gun trio slewed around in their saddles, taken completely off guard. Instantly Cheeko's sixgun bellowed and the nearest of the three grabbed his shoulder and crashed heavily to the ground. Raging and whiskey-brave, his henchmen raked with spur and went charging headlong for the alley, filling the dark mouth with a fusillade of shots that brought down a broken gate and put finish to Mama Pollygene's big front window in a shimmering shower of tinkling glass.

But the closest that lethal volley came to their quarry was to splinter the corner boards of the Billiard Parlor where he'd momentarily appeared.

The two were reining in as Cheeko's gun stormed from another angle. The man was greased lightning, as Marshal Cardinal knew. The second rider sagged in the saddle and tried desperately to hold on, might have managed it had not his horse suddenly collapsed beneath him with a .45 slug in the heart.

The sole survivor whacked his horse with his hat and stormed out of Tincup with bullets whistling murderously close, his mouth stretching in a silent grimace of pure terror when something white hot and agonizing clipped the curve of his shoulder and almost brought him out of the saddle.

Then the corner loomed, he was round it like a shot and all that followed him on his headlong flight from town was the fading sound of Cheeko's mocking laughter.

Paiute customers watched breathlessly as Cheeko swaggered from cover, a smoking cutter in either hand, cowboy hat thrust back from his ugly young face. He housed one gun then ostentatiously cocked the other as he turned theatrically to stare across fifty feet of street to where a pathetic figure on all fours was dragging a shattered leg after him as he crawled for an alley-mouth.

Billy Cheeko's laugh rang clear on the night air.

'Charlie, Charlie,' he mocked, 'go easy on yourself. You know you just gotta die, boys.'

'No, they don't. Drop those cutters, scum!'

Cheeko whirled and there was the marshal, gun in hand, six feet tall, brass badge gleaming, face in shadow. Mr Marshal Cardinal in the flesh!

'Bastard!' white-faced Cheeko screamed. The gun in his hand leapt upwards and fire and smoke billowed from Cardinal's waist as he triggered twice at this outlaw who had shot a man in his city.

Cheeko fell forward on his face. Cardinal dumped shells from his smoking gun and ran slitted eyes over the town. It seemed to take forever for the harsh echoes of those final shots to beat into silence across the shadow-rumpled prairies beyond the town.

The lawman showed no emotion as he moved forward again. He had not one but three wounded to tend to. He hoped the doctor wasn't too drunk.

The Storytown that Gene Cardinal ruled was one of the Territory's fastest growing centers in the decade following the Civil War. With its population now stretching past the ten thousand mark, it was a rising power in industry and commerce. Headquarters of the booming Grand West Railroad and straddling the Key River, tributary of the Arkansas, Storytown was a mecca for the go-getters, empire-builders and visionaries of the Seventies.

Cattle kings from Texas and Kansas, mining tycoons from New Mexico and Wyoming and magnates in timber, iron, wool, beef and transport met and mingled here on tree-lined Frontier Square.

They transacted their affairs and hatched big deals in oak-paneled saloons, the more opulent hotels and did not overlook the Parisian splendours of the more elegant salons fronting notorious Dixie Street, that storied thoroughfare which ran all the way from the handsome falsefronts of the square down to the levees on the Key a mile distant.

This was a city where the money was made, and where there was money there were always those tempted to rob, defraud, extort, connive and even kill to get their hands on it the quickest way possible – hence ten deputies and a marshal.

When the deputy strength of the imposing law and court offices, set back from Plains Street off the square, was raised from seven to ten, following the Jackson Gang shootout eighteen months earlier, even some pro law and order voices such as the newspapers and the Christian Women's League thought the council might be going a little too far too fast.

'Ten deputies!' the chairwoman of the straight-laced League had protested. 'Good Lord, what sort of picture will this paint of us to the outside world? They will have no choice but to believe that any city on the plains which is prepared to pay good money for ten deputies must perforce need ten deputies!'

That was a year and a half ago. Nobody complained about the drain on the civic purse occasioned by ten deputies and one highly paid marshal being on the payroll any longer.

Luke Parradine and a parade of lesser criminals had taken care of that.

Parradine was the wild man from the distant Rockies who'd attempted to mastermind and execute a twenty-man attack on the Buell Bank a year back, a bloody incident which left Parradine, three of his hellers and two brave deputies dead in the dust of Frontier Square, casualties of Marshal Cardinal's police work and smoking guns.

Whilst boosting the marshal's stock sky high, the Parradine affair had the unfortunate side effect of convincing other like minded malefactors that big-time Storytown was now a rich place, well worth the robbing – if only a man had the balls to try.

Snitch Preston, The Missouri Bunch, Cole Waller, the Clanton Brothers and more recently one Billy Cheeko had all in turn attempted to succeed where Parradine failed. The result? More graves in Boot Hill, several new faces at the jailhouse and the vaults of the city's three main banks unbreached.

Before Cheeko made his attempt on the Deposit Bank's armoured coach the previous week, it had been four months since serious crime had visited Storytown. And with Cheeko and the Jacksons already tried, sentenced and en route to Territory Prison this morning, Gene Cardinal was greeted like the most popular peace officer in the West as he made his rounds with Slow Joe Pierce.

'Congrats, Marshal, we knew you'd nail that one.'

'Hey, Marshal Cardinal, just want you to know all of us on the railroad are mighty proud of the way you make it easy for us to work and live without lookin' over our shoulders for train-jumpers and road agents.'

Although he privately regarded such public acclaim as unwelcome, the sober lawman responded to them as gravely and respectfully as he did to the more acceptable nods and smiles.

For someone who had spent the past decade in the harsh glare of the town-taming profession, Cardinal was a reserved and private man who would avoid the limelight where possible, yet by the same token was prepared to have his likeness plastered across all the newspapers of the West if that succeeded in warning the scum away from his town. At times like this he was lucky to have Slow Joe along with him, for as formal and at times taciturn as the marshal of Storytown might be, his right hand man was almost the direct opposite, as the responses from the citizens they encountered demonstrated.

'Thank you, Miz Callahan, we just try to do our best – but don't forget your donation to the Law Office Fund, will you?' And, 'Sorry I had to cut loose and gun some of those wasters down up at the Paiute. But they had it comin', and if you want to hand the credit to the marshal here, heck, I'm a modest man with plenty to be modest about, you might say.'

Cardinal didn't know how he did it. Cynical and sardonic, the weather-ravaged Pierce had the ability to treat everyone pretty much alike be they tycoon or two-fisted tough; cattle king or shyster; a visiting Washington senator or some shot-up no-good like Billy Cheeko.

Not him.

Cardinal walked in a black and white world. If you were honest and straight, you were his friend; if tainted by the owlhoot, the enemy.

That was how he operated. It had worked in other places and was working here in Storytown on the Territory's western prairies.

When he made the late morning rounds with Slow Joe and saw at first hand the benefits of the law regime he'd implemented in this place, Cardinal felt good. He'd taken risks in the Paiute operation in Tincup but they'd paid off handsomely. Another dog pack taken out of the equation and the supremacy of law and order reaffirmed.

At a time like this a man could relax, suck in some good clean air and even bask a little in the approval of the people he represented.

But it didn't last, couldn't last.

It was while the two lawmen were taking coffee at the Hot Pot coffee house on North, reviewing the day's agenda and with Pierce trying to flirt with the new waitress half his age that the marshal of Storytown was given a reminder that a man might do well enough in the eyes of most, most of the time, but never with everybody; with some citizens, never.

The man who emerged from a room in back was around forty, fat and florid in an all-white suit and yet you sensed, hard. Emil Branco ran the Mogul Saloon as well as having fingers sunk in many a commercial pie. Brash, self-assured and full of himself, Branco was a power in the city but not one happy or able to work in conjunction with the Cardinal law regime.

The men had been at odds ever since the marshal's controversial appointment. Branco regarded Cardinal as a glory-hunting autocrat while in return the marshal saw the big man as a half-and-half, bluff, booming and respectable in the eyes of most yet a man you sensed was capable of most anything in the holy cause of achieving what he wanted.

Wreathed in a cloud of cigar smoke, Branco halted on sighting the pair perched on high stools at the side counter.

Customers paused to watch. The so-called Branco versus lawhouse feud was common knowledge on the streets and it was not unusual for sparks to fly when they met.

'Sorry, Marshal.' Branco's voice was rich and fruity, tinged today with sarcasm.

'What?' Cardinal was stern. At six feet two with a broad-shouldered and long-legged build, he was an impressive man of thirty who rarely smiled and whose manner usually only radiated so much warmth. It was all serious to Gene Cardinal. He rarely saw the humorous side of law enforcement, as Slow Joe most always did. In his rigid way, if he could not classify this man as pro law and above suspicion, then that made him a suspect, one hundred dollar suits and thriving business enterprises notwithstanding.

Branco approached, walking in that bouncy way short and overweight men often exhibit.

'I didn't get around to stopping by and adding my voice to the Greek chorus of praise I hear you've rated after yesterday's shooting business in the Paiute. Sorry about that – Marshal.'

The lawmen traded looks. The deputy slid off his stool, rugged, compact, seam-faced and unsmiling.

'Anyone ever tell you you're full of shit, Branco?'

Cardinal put a hand on the deputy's arm as the

15

saloonman flushed hotly.

'Take it easy, Slow Joe. Mr Branco likes to run off at the mouth. You should know that.'

'Seems a taxpayer can't pass a compliment around here without having two-bit tinstars jumping all over him,' Branco said, eyes cut to slits. 'You know, Marshal, your, what we might call, top-lofty ways might be rubbing off on your hired hands. I can remember when old Slow Joe here was a halfway amusing kind of fellow. Not over smart, wouldn't go that far, but sociable enough. See how he's changed.'

'What's on your mind, Branco?' Cardinal challenged.

The fat man dragged deeply on his cigar. 'I'm told you're looking to close down my place on Dixie, Cardinal, that is what's on my mind,' he said toughly. 'Only heard about it while you were off glory-hunting. I'd like to hear there's no truth in it.'

'I've warned you often enough about the games your men operate at the Sweet Julep,' Cardinal stated flatly. 'I'm halfway to being able to prove your dealers augment their luck, and the day I do that I'll lock those doors and throw away the key.'

'You hear that?' Branco shouted angrily, the sweeping gesture he made with his white planter's hat inviting the clientele to witness what was said. 'A sworn-in city marshal threatening a respectable citizen in broad daylight. Is that what we pay this man a king's ransom for? Shooting up anyone he

16

doesn't like and trying to drive honest folk out of business?'

'Take it easy,' the marshal counseled.

But Emil Branco wasn't listening. He'd made his grandstand play, had shown again that he was not afraid to stand up to the formidable marshal, chose to storm out of the place waving his hat and inviting startled customers to wake up to what was going on in their town before it was too late.

Gene Cardinal spun a coin on the counter and the lawmen walked out into the sunlight, where life was flowing through the streets of Storytown.

The easy morning was in back of them. The Branco incident was a reminder that the supremacy he was seeking to establish over the troublesome factions here was still a long way from total.

Storytown had had one of the worst reputations in the Territory prior to Cardinal's appointment. And as though Branco's outburst had served to unlock the underlying lawlessness, before they got back to the law office they were obliged to step in and stop a fight amongst a bunch of teamsters at the Arkansas Avenue freight depot and then they arrested a drunk for strong-arming an oldtimer on Dixie.

Another day in Storytown was underway. Already the dust was riding, the eternal dust of the big plains city. Throughout the afternoon it would mingle with loco smoke from the switching yards until the town was dust- and heat-hazed, and blurred out of focus.

Quincey Halstrom's water wagon, groaning and creaking from the weight of its rusted red tank, moved sluggishly about Frontier Square, spraying water in back of it.

But the city's dust was never laid for long. Like its lawless streak, it was always ready to rise again. Soon it would be whipped up by boot-heels, steel-shod hoofs and iron-bound wheels. It would hang in the air until it drifted back down, in an unending haze across to the jail and lawhouse, the imposing Town Hall and the huge, shabby old general store which occupied almost one full side of the square. It fell indiscriminately upon the gleaming new railroad and the imposing façades of the Mogul Saloon, the Plainsman Hotel and the crib-lined slum streets running off Lower Dixie down by the broad brown snake of the river.

The eternal dust of Storytown was churned up by the wheels of industry. But while many men were making big deals, doing business and raking in their honest rewards, the other kind were also busy – the crooks, the panhandlers, the con artists and the hard-knuckled bar-room brawlers and all the broken men.

And the marshal's deputies gathered them in that day as they did every day of the week, and after nightfall all would appear in the show-up room in the sprawling jailhouse to be assessed, charged, or set free.

It was an unusual fact of life in a bustling city which boasted an opera house and a healthy theater, not to mention all the amusements and distractions at dozens of saloons, dance halls, gambling establishments and bordellos, that the line-ups that took place three nights a week at Cardinal's jailhouse, with Slow Joe Pierce presiding, were rated by many as the best show in town. . . .

CHAPTER 2

LADY FROM DODGE

'Where did you get that switchblade, farmer?'

'A lady friend asked me to mind it for her, Deputy, honest to God.'

'Tell that to your mule and he'll kick your head in. Next!'

Next in line at the show-up room was an old stew bum with a battered face the texture of old adobe, squinting painfully on account of the bright lights burning down before Slow Joe's scarred desk.

'What did they arrest you for, Pete?'

'I just stole a ounce of chaw terbaccer.'

'You ought to be ashamed of yourself. One ounce? Next time steal a crate and do it right. Take him down!'

A murmur ran through the onlookers, voices laced with soft laughter. Deputy Pierce was in good form tonight, they told one another. And waited for the next loser to be paraded before the charge table in order that they might witness just how low their fellow man could sink, what outrageous lies they might spin in their desperate attempt to avoid being fined, sentenced to several days' detention right here at the law headquarters, or worst of all, be dispatched to County Prison.

'What'd you do, Charlie?'

'Lord love us, Deputy, all I done was stopped to help an old lady up.'

'You helped her up by her pocketbook. Get him out of here. Next!'

They were brought in off the streets, from the dives and the clip joints. They were picked up from trains, raided in hobo jungles out along the tracks, scooped up wherever Marshal Cardinal's wide net stretched; sunburned cow thieves; pale-complexioned gunkids looking only to make a name; the brutal, the pitiful and the just plain no-good.

Each had his moment beneath those harsh lights, one brief slice of time in the limelight to state his case and pray for compassion. And, as always, there was an audience to see how they fared.

It had been the marshal's decision to move the show-up room to the courthouse adjoining the law office. From the outset, he wanted due process to be open and above suspicion following years of highly suspect enforcement here. For some, these nightly events were sometimes regarded as a kind of entertainment, particularly when Slow Joe Pierce was running things.

'James Hortland Prentice, your Honor Deputy Pierce, sir.'

'Just call me Nemesis, loser. Why were you wrongly arrested, Mr Prentice?'

'I stole a dog, sir.'

Pierce looked around. 'Er, does that come under the headin' of rustling, Marshal?'

All heads turned towards Gene Cardinal seated to one side beyond the glare of the overhead lights. Occasionally Pierce would involve him in this street theater ritual in the hope of drawing a smile or some kind of appreciation for his acerbic wit. But tonight the marshal of Storytown failed to respond, even though a titter of amusement was still rippling through the oddly assorted crowd of society women, hardcases, high-steppers and their brassy women, some of them just as strange and flawed as those they had come to see.

'Get on with it, Deputy,' was the marshal's only response, and Pierce dutifully did just that.

'What have you been doing since you appeared here last, you hangdog heel thief?'

'Why, I been workin', Deputy.'

'What at?'

'I'm a cook.'

'You couldn't cook water for a barber. Get him out of here.'

Until finally it was almost a welcome relief to see a genuine hardcase emerge from the ruck of deadbeats and dognappers to stand four-square before that table. He was a slim-hipped, cold-eyed, bayonet of a man, standing chin up, shoulders squared, not yet twenty-one, yet as old as any man in town.

'Better make it good, Shelley. You're charged here with stabbing a man in a fight at the Sweet Julep.'

'It's plain I never done it, you broken-winded old goat.'

The crowd leaned forward, the line-up was hushed. Few dared take Slow Joe Pierce on here, where for an hour or two, three nights a week, he was the lawman most in the limelight in Storytown.

'You'll have to explain, son.'

'If I'd run a blade into the son of a bitch he'd be in the mortuary by this time.'

Nobody sniggered now, and Cardinal leaned forward on his chair to study the prisoner more closely. His eyes were intent and he was wondering as he sometimes did, if this might be just another hot-shot punk kid with big ideas about himself, or if he might prove to be a genuinely dangerous man in the making.

Cardinal was fascinated by the criminal mind, too much so according to some. His admirers regarded this trait as proof of his total commitment to his profession, but others were less generous. The latter contended that the marshal's harsh attitude to lawbreakers was almost obsessive at times. Both factions would have been surprised and perhaps shocked to learn the truth of it, which was something the marshal kept to himself.

'What are you starin' at, wonder man?' Shelley hissed.

Cardinal rose and approached the man, who stiffened. He stared into his eyes and young Ike Shelley flinched, almost intimidated by that hard stare.

'You could be grooming yourself for big troubles, Shelley. You are smart-mouthed and stupid, but worst of all you are a criminal. You stabbed that citizen sure enough and you botched it, just as you are botching your life. A month in County, that's what I'll be recommending to the judge for you. Next offence and it will be five years.'

'You can't do that.'

'It's done. Take him down.'

Before the deputies could reach them, Shelley cursed and swung a punch. Cardinal parried then delivered a short jolting hook to the jaw that sent the man staggering back into the arms of the deputies, glassy-eyed, tongue lolling.

'Two months, for the attempted assault upon a law officer,' Cardinal told Slow Joe as the man was hauled away, toes dragging on the floorboards. 'Next!'

That incident helped make it a fine night for the spectators, and when it was all over and the show-up room was slowly clearing, two members of the Christian Women's League sought out the marshal to express their appreciation of what he was doing in making their city a safe and proper place to live.

Gathering up his material nearby, Pierce paused, watching.

He had a suspicion the wealthy widow might have her eye on the marshal, while Janet Julian, wife of the mayor and matriarch of city society, could be almost embarrassingly attentive and flattering in the lawman's company. He started towards the group but Gene motioned him back. Socializing with the citizenry was at times an obligation for the marshal. Besides, Widow Carlotta Roebuck was a genuine looker in an ice princess kind of way.

'You really must give us a date when you can address the League, Marshal Cardinal,' gushed the mayor's wife.

'Only if Mrs Roebuck agrees to bake one of her sponge cakes,' Cardinal replied, giving a small bow.

He liked the way the woman's face lit up, so he allowed himself to stay chatting for several minutes longer. Yet his heart wasn't in it. Tonight, the marshal wanted to be alone and eventually got his wish after the last visitor left and he'd declined to join the deputies for a nightcap at Jake's Bar.

The lights were low and the marshal stood with one boot up on a chair, elbow on his knee, jaw resting on his fist.

All the troublemakers were gone, either back to the freedom of the streets or downstairs into the underground holding cells pending appearance before the judge next morning. Yet it seemed to him here in this pale shifting light that he could still hear the shuffling steps and the hopeful pleas of every rogue and wagon grifter, every shakedown artist, sneak thief, cattle rustler plus all the cat burglars and extortionists as they made their pleas;

'I didn't do it. . . . It was just a coincidence I was in that alley. . . . She hit me first and all I done was hit back. . . .'

He shook his head. Sometimes it seemed that in his life, dealing with guilt every waking hour, he felt almost guilty himself. Guilty because of his righteousness, his punitive way of dealing with them, the top-lofty way he held himself above them like some grim Judge of Heaven. Until their guilt and his guilt melded together and Gene Cardinal could feel as though it was he standing beneath those harsh lights, squinting to find his accusers' faces as they charged him with the offence of considering himself better than they. . . .

His boot came down to the floor with a bang and he turned for the exit. Times like this he knew he was too involved with his work and as a consequence got to see far too much of the outlaw side of life than any man rightly should.

Of course know-all Slow Joe reckoned he knew the solution to his situation, just as he believed he was the only one qualified to decide who should go back to freedom and who should go down the stairs to the cells.

A good woman, marriage, and quit working sixteen hours a day. Simple!

Gene Cardinal rejected the simple solution of finding a woman who would look after him and eventually become more important than his career.

Tried that. Hadn't worked.

And turning out the last light, he quit the darkened building and leaned wearily into the night.

Five passengers disembarked from the noon stage from the south-east but only one seemed worthy of attention as far as the hands at the stage depot were concerned. They were jostling to take charge of the dark lady's luggage, ignoring the glares of the drummer, the banker, the fish oil salesman from Tacoma and even those of the plump and petulant wife of Storytown's share broker when she was welcomed back by several of her more important friends, including the mayor's wife.

She was not a lady to accept irritation uncomplainingly.

'Just look at her, will you,' she hissed to her welcoming committee, all dressed in taffeta and sheltered by floral sun brollies. 'Just look at her – playing up to everything in trousers just as she was aboard the stage, shameless hussy. Here, you, young Bixley. I also have luggage you might notice, if you could take your time to put your eyes back into their sockets.'

Young Bixley didn't even seem to hear. He had hold of one of the dark lady's satchels and was hanging onto it for all he was worth while the hatbox, valise and carry-bag of the sharebroker's wife stood ignored on the deck.

'Really!' the good woman protested and moved her smelling salts beneath her large fleshy nose. 'Have you ever seen anything like it?'

But the ladies were too interested in the new arrival to pay her much attention. For she was very striking. She exhibited the sinuous grace of a dancer as she moved about the landing regally, asking questions, issuing orders and occasionally flashing a smile which seemed to light up the depot as though the sun had just come out from behind a cloud.

Curiosity and disapproval marked the faces of the mayor's wife's retinue. Plainly the young woman was too showy and sure of herself to be one of them, yet obviously had too much class about her to be totally dismissed.

'Is she in business?' enquired the widow Roebuck. 'I rather sense she might be.' She could afford to be superior about women in business. Her jewel-dealer husband had shuffled off leaving her a mansion and a sack of precious stones you could stun a bighorn sheep with, in the process rendering her about the most eligible woman in town.

The plump lady showed some hint of malicious satisfaction. 'Saloons.'

'Saloons?' The mayor's wife was shocked. 'You mean she deals in them, buying and selling?'

'Operating,' the fat lady supplied. And that was the end of interest in Rebecca Winters so far as this cross section of Storytown's upper class was concerned. But certainly this did not apply to the menfolk present.

Every man seemed only too eager to escort the newcomer along to the hotel. And they did. All of them. So it was that Rebecca Winters made her dramatic entrance to that establishment at the

28

head of an entourage of no less than seven males including the stage company boss who was clutching her hatbox as though it contained the crown jewels.

In a corner of the lobby, Slow Joe Pierce was deliberately leaning on the third waistcoat button of a dandy gambler from the Rockies who was turning pale because the pressure on his sternum from a big spatulate forefinger was interfering with his breathing.

There was the matter of a card game at the Boxed Dice gambling house on Arkansas Avenue the previous night in which a gentleman answering this gambler's description had apparently produced five aces in a high stake game.

Pierce was interrogating his man when the commotion at the doors drew his attention. He flicked a glance towards the party, turned back to his man, did a double take then swung around fully just as the beauty breasted the counter and enquired after the best room in the house. 'Judas!' gasped the deputy, and was out the side door before the rumpled gambler from the Rockies had fully caught his breath.

'Imagine running from something like that!' the cardsharp muttered, straightening his necktie. 'Always thought there was something queer about that block-headed lawdog.'

Then he headed for the clerk's desk, putting on his best smile. He rated himself something of a ladies' man and classified this raven-headed beauty as A-grade prime.

The marshal's ex-lover had shown up in town!

This was the hot news that swept across Frontier Square and hurried from salon to saloon, from railroad depot to cracker-barrel store and gambling club all along Walnut, North, Arkansas and made its way brushfire quick down Dixie Street all the way to the levee and the riverboats in record time.

Her name was said to be Rebecca Winters and the well-publicized romance had blossomed in Dodge City where a wounded Cardinal had been laid up for several months after putting the lid on Channahan, South Dakota.

Although further details proved skimpy, it was believed in some quarters that the marshal and Miss Winters had parted on anything but amicable terms. Indeed a rumor, reputedly emanating from the law office itself, had it that so dramatic had the big breakup been that Marshal Cardinal had sworn off women for life.

Naturally all the gossips from Republican Circle all the way down to the river were craving for more information to feed their curiosity, but came up mostly empty. None knew Rebecca Winters well enough to justify quizzing her on her personal affairs just yet, and certainly none dared question the marshal on the subject. As far as could be determined, the only other citizen who might be in a position to cast light on the affair in Dodge City was Slow Joe Pierce, and he simply wasn't talking.

But the first deputy was thinking plenty in the late afternoon of the same day as he he set off for a solitary patrol along North and Walnut, with the low lying sun cutting deep, black shadows across the road.

'Hi there, Deputy,' greeted a rum-ruined face vaguely familiar to Pierce from a line-up. 'Much obliged for you givin' me the benefit of the doubt and settin' me loose again last night.'

'Get lost before I collar you again and throw the book at you, boozehound.'

The man's face fell. He was so shocked he was tempted to shout a retort after the lawman but thought better of it.

Smart citizen.

For the deputy was riding an edge today, was prickly, uneasy and kept stopping to massage the back of his neck, a sure sign of tension.

There was no prize for guessing why.

While Rebecca Winters was as striking a female as Slow Joe had ever clapped eyes upon, he was anything but pleased to see her striding the streets of Storytown like a celebrity from the richer side of Boston. And when dusk found him making his way back along Dixie, and he again sighted the woman in the company of Emil Branco, inspecting the old French Palace which had been closed with a FOR SALE sign out front for some months, he decided that instead of chewing on his liver with apprehension he should simply bite the bullet and go to find out just what she was doing here and how long she meant to stay.

To his surprise he found Miss Winters taking a solitary supper in the gleaming dining room of her plush hotel, The Clairmont, an hour later.

Pierce had spruced himself up for the meeting, running a razor over his deeply lined visage for the second time that day, damped and combed down his hair, even donned a freshly laundered dark blue shirt and dressed it up with a handsome silver-ornamented bola.

Storytown's first deputy was not seeking to impress ; he simply wanted to make a good impression in the hope it might smooth over the brief association they'd once had, which had never been better than prickly.

He might have saved himself the trouble; later he told himself he could have had a two-hour soak at Mother Mulroney's bath-house and doused himself in lavender water and it still would have made no difference.

Black eyelashes snapped at him; there was certainly no hint of Rebecca Winters's famous smile to be seen.

'What do you want, Slowpoke?'

'Slow Joe.'

'Whatever.' The woman speared a stick of asparagus dextrously with a silver fork and popped the morsel prettily into her mouth. 'Did Gene send you?'

'Nope, he didn't. Haven't seen him since you showed, to tell the truth.'

'So you came to see me of your own volition?'

'You could put it that way.'

Rebecca set down her fork, dabbed at the corners of her mouth with a burgundy napkin then leaned back in her chair allowing her gaze to play over the room. The Clairmont's dining rooms were well patronised tonight, largely by the more affluent class, most of whom appeared to be watching, either slyly or overtly, what was taking place at her table.

This did not bother her. She was accustomed to attention. What disturbed her was this squat, sad-featured man with the star on his chest shifting from one foot to the other as he stood before her table.

'For a man who has practically made a career out of running off at the mouth, you seem almost tongue-tied, Slowpoke.'

'Don't you feel you've given Gene enough grief, lady?' That came out more bluntly than he'd intended, but it was certainly clear and to the point. 'After Dodge, I mean.'

'So,' she said after a short silence, 'I see in a year and a half nothing has changed. Gene is, I gather, still playing God, while you are still his gofer and lap dog.' A winged eyebrow arched high. 'That is how it is, isn't it, Deputy Slowpoke?'

His seamed face set harder. 'I'm still loyal to the man if that is what you mean. More than I can say for some.'

'All right,' she snapped with an air of finality, 'that does it. You've worn out your welcome, you're annoying me, so kindly disappear before I call the law.'

'I am the law.'

She met his eyes levelly, spoke softly. 'You are nothing.'

It had always been like this, back in Dodge City. They had been at loggerheads from the outset, Pierce over-protective of the man he served, Rebecca resenting the deputy's attitude towards her. They had never hit it off, and when the big break came between her and Cardinal, Pierce had been there to tell the marshal 'I told you so'. Then helped him pack, leaving behind Dodge City, Miss Rebecca Winters and her new lover.

He turned and walked out, heavy-footed and with a long face filled with foreboding. Slow Joe Pierce, the show-up room boss who always looked for the worst in the endless parade of villains and misfits who came before him, could see nothing but big trouble ahead at this turn of events.

He went looking for the marshal only to find Cardinal involved with other troubles.

CHAPTER 3

MAN ON THE RUN

Cardinal's face was grim.

'How bad?' he demanded of the lathered cowboy. 'Come on, come on, man. Kendle? How bad is he hurt?'

The Lazy X waddy turned his hat in his hands. The marshal made him nervous, always did. He cleared his throat and said, 'I . . . I gotta tell you, Marshal Cardinal sir. That dude is dead – shot in the back, and dead.'

It was suddenly quiet in the law office. The noise of a wagon passing by outside sounded unnaturally loud. Cardinal continued to stare at the pale cowboy. For good reason he hesitated a long moment before posing the question he didn't want to ask.

'Who shot Kendle?'

The cowboy swallowed.

'Guess it was Mr Slater, Marshal.'

Cardinal's face turned cold. He and the eccentric and volatile rancher were friends who went back quite a way. Harry Slater had come to see him when he first had wife troubles. He hadn't been able to help him. Now the new hand Slater had accused of carrying on with his wife had been shot dead out at Lazy X.

'Just . . . just tell me what happened, cowboy. . . .'

The story didn't take long to tell. It seemed Kendle had been simply strolling in the rose garden at dusk when a shot rang out and he fell dead. When Slater showed up, his hysterical wife straightaway accused him of murder. There had been a big fight after that and some confusion. Slater had eventually fled the headquarters on horseback when his wife ordered Billy Buck to ride into Storytown and report the murder.

'Mr Slater?' Cardinal said at length. 'Was Mr Slater hurt in the fracas?'

'Well, no sir, Marshal Cardinal,' the man said uncomfortably. 'I mean . . . well, the way we figured, Mr Slater was doin' the shootin' and Mr Kendle was the one stoppin' the lead. So. . . .'

'Did anyone see Harry do the shooting?'

'Not as I know of, Marshal.'

All eyes were on Cardinal as he stood motionless staring at the cowboy. It was common knowledge that he and the eccentric ranch boss of the Lazy X were close. Now the lawman was being told that his friend was alleged to have shot a man down in cold blood out there.

Not just any man either.

The curse of wild gossip thrived in Storytown as it did in most large range towns, and the rumor that flashy Errol Kendle and Mrs Muriel Slater were enjoying an illicit rangeland romance out on the big spread had been gaining wide currency of late. Hence there was little doubt as to what everybody in that room was thinking right now.

With the exception of the man sporting the marshal's badge, that was.

Mayor Dory Julian, always quick to show up at the first whiff of trouble, bent a hard stare on Cardinal. He was about to speak when the door swung inwards and Slow Joe Pierce came in, a little short of breath.

'Is it true what I hear, Marshal. . . ?' he began, then paused as he studied the faces. He nodded, 'Uh huh, guess it is.' He turned to his superior again. 'Is it as bad as it sounds, boss?'

'That's to be decided,' Cardinal replied, moving to the rack and taking down his Stetson hat. 'So far as the cowboy knows, nobody actually saw the shooting – they just heard the shot and Kendle fell dead with a bullet through his back.'

'Had to happen sooner or later, I guess.' The mayor was a successful supplies agent who liked to believe he always kept his finger on the county's pulse. He caught Cardinal's warning glare and spread his hands wide. 'Hell, Marshal, I'm only saying what everybody'll say. We've been hearing that rancher lady's been carryin' on with her fancy man on and off for weeks. Guess Harry just upped and decided he'd had enough, and I can't say I blame him.'

Making for the door, Cardinal 'accidentally' brushed shoulders with the storekeeper and almost knocked the man off his feet. Julian swore and Cardinal pivoted and shoved a finger under his nose.

'No language in my office, mister. Now, if you don't have any legitimate business here then get the hell out. *Sabe?*'

Pale-faced and furious, the mayor hustled out leaving Slow Joe studying his superior warily.

'You plan to mosey on out there I figger, Marshal?'

'I'm on my way.'

'Want some company?'

'No – yes.'

'Er, is that a yes or a—'

'Go get your horse, damnit!' Cardinal was not ordinarily this testy but this was no ordinary situation. As the deputy hurried out the rear door he turned to second deputy Bob Walker. 'You'll be in charge while we're gone, Bob. Anything on the blotter can wait until we get back.'

Without waiting for a reply, he swung out to find a small crowd had already assembled out front by the tierack.

'Break it up,' he barked, jumping down into the dust. 'Be about your business or I'll book you all for loitering.'

They scattered, but had reassembled on the gallery of the hotel opposite by the time Cardinal and Pierce emerged mounted from the lane flanking the law office and headed off along the street at the lope.

'Danged difficult man that Marshal Cardinal,' complained the mayor. 'You'd reckon we were the criminals, not his pal, Slater.'

'Heck, we don't know Slater shot that feller yet, Mr Mayor,' the blacksmith protested. 'Mebbe, but it looks bad and—'

'Oh, I reckon we'll find he killed the man right enough,' Julian overrode him. 'And I can't say I blame him. . . .'

Heads nodded all around and the mayor nodded his head emphatically. He plainly had Harry Slater tried, convicted and sentenced already, and judging by the sober faces all around him, most of Storytown shared his sentiments.

It wasn't a pretty sight, a healthy thirty-year-old man shot to death and now lying stiff and stark on a plank bench in the barn.

The bullet had entered Kendle's back, shattering his backbone and catching the heart before exiting.

'What did you see, Muriel?' Cardinal asked sternly.

The tearful woman shrugged and related the story that coincided in all respects with what he'd already been told by the cowboy.

'I believe you reckon Harry did the shooting?' he pressed.

'Who else could have, Gene? Who else had any reason to do such a dreadful thing?'

'Do you have any notion where he might have gone?'

'Well, you know my husband. He was always wandering off someplace, hadn't been settled in some time.'

Cardinal could understand that. Harry was an old-fashioned man, straight as a gunbarrel. If his wife had been carrying on with the dead man it stood to reason he might be a little unsettled.

Outside, he set Slow Joe and the hands to searching the headquarters area from end to end. After an hour he came up with a set of bootprints by the well that didn't match those of any man on the place. Big bootprints. They scanned the surrounds by lanternlight but by midnight he called a halt, realizing they weren't likely to find anything further amongst all the man and horse tracks around the headquarters.

He drank down a pannikin of scalding hot coffee enlivened by a jolt from his hip flask before quitting the Lazy X with a new deputy, young Owen Placer, in near total darkness. He paid no attention to sign as they crossed to the boundary then took the old canyon trail. Placer kept glancing at him questioningly as they followed the sharply rising trail but Cardinal rode grimly with his gaze fixed ahead, confiding nothing at this stage.

Monument Rocks was a geographically wild region in sharp contrast to the rangelands spread around its massive fringes. He'd done some hunting with Slater in the Rocks region in the past, and it was exactly the kind of country he would make for if he found himself in big trouble.

And at first glance, that was where Harry Slater was right now. Big trouble in the eyes of everyone who counted, including his lady wife.

Everyone, most likely, but Sheriff Gene Cardinal.

He realized he was biased in Slater's favor. But deep down he would never believe his friend could dry-gulch a man, killing him stone dead, until he was confronted by the kind of proof that might convince any judge and jury in the land of his guilt.

At two thousand feet, the pre-dawn air cut like an Apache scalp axe. Cardinal rubbed his hands briskly then blew upon them, visible breath fog squeezing between his fingers.

The sky was clear to the east indicating a fine day coming, and it couldn't come too soon to suit the deputy.

'S-see anything yet, Marshal?'

'No, and I don't expect to. Or at least not until full light.'

Thirty minutes later the feeble sun winked on the horizon and Monument Rocks loomed huge before them, a mighty tumbling landscape of cliffs, ravines, tremendous thrusting escarpments and soaring ridges.

And still no sign of life anyplace but for a solitary early-morning eagle searching for a rising thermal above Mount Puerto.

The sudden blast of a revolver almost caused the deputy to lose balance. He staggered then looked back incredulously at the smoke plume rising from Cardinal's sixgun barrel.

'Jumping Judas Priest, Marshal! What the hell—?'

He got no further. Cardinal filled his lungs and shouted; 'Harry, it's me, Gene! I know you're up there someplace – on Yellow Ledge if I'm any guess. Better come on down, pard. If I can find you anyone can . . . so let me see you!'

Silence.

The deputy built a cigarette and set it alight, eyes on the massive landscape. The horses acted nervous in the echoing stillness.

'Harry, I'm waiting!'

Still nothing.

Five minutes passed. Ten. By now the sun was clear of the broken stone mountain and the county was spread below them in all its vastness, rolling all the way to the blob of color along the river that was the town, then onwards into infinity.

And still no response or any sign of life in all this world of stone; even the eagle had vacated the sky.

'What now, Marshal Cardinal?'

'Why, what now is that you get it easy, Deputy,' Cardinal replied, drawing his Winchester .32 from the saddle scabbard. 'Mind the horses, keep sharp, and if you need me back here for any reason touch off two quick shots in succession. *Sabe?*'

Placer nodded dumbly. It was his first visit to the rocks region and he was spooked by its titanic strangeness and the whispering silence. Why would a man want to hide out here? If he was in Harry Slater's boots he'd be taking his chances by riding across the county line and heading for the border – any damned border anyplace would do.

An hour later found Cardinal a further thousand feet higher. The sun was warming the big country below but up here it was growing even colder. He paid no mind to stiff fingers or rasping breath. He was fully aware that if Slater had taken off in any other direction he would be well and truly gone by the time he was forced to acknowledge his mistake. That would also entail his having to admit that he was reading his friend wrong, and that wasn't something he would enjoy. After clambering up and over a steepled rock face to gain a broad yellow ledge of time-worn granite, he was standing with hands on hips, blowing hard and catching his breath when he stiffened. Directly before him in clear sight in a patch of trapped sand was the distinct outline of a footprint.

It was pointing west in the general direction of Yellow Step Ledge, where he was heading. Where he and Harry had camped once hunting bear! He was about to congratulatulate himself for his prescience when understanding hit.

It was not Slater's footprint, yet was somehow familiar.

He stiffened as recognition hit.

These were the same big prints he'd discovered by the hand pump back at the ranch headquarters!

He jerked his head up, Colt filling his hand. Suddenly the surrounding tumble of talus seemed alive with menace. After a minute of silence the tension began to ease somewhat.

But this was still going to take some figuring. No sign of Harry, yet almost certainly the man he reckoned could well prove to be the killer was up here ... maybe waiting for him in ambush around the next corner.

Why?

Was the man looking to hole up here in the Crocker Range? Or could he be, like him, searching for a scared and on-the-run Harry Slater?

As he turned the sun caught his star and winked brightly. An instant later the mighty silences were shattered by the snarling crash of a rifle and he was diving headlong with the sounds of a vicious ricochet howling in his ears.

He kicked beneath an overhang and waited. A thousand feet below, a jittery deputy was staring upwards but saw nothing, not even a wisp of gunsmoke.

Silence.

Cardinal was belly-wriggling cautiously ahead when the shout came tumbling down over the awesome stone façade, 'Gene! Gene, are you OK?'

Harry's voice!

'Yeah, Harry—' he roared but his voice was swallowed instantly by the booming roar of a rifle from somewhere close.

The bullet smacked the ledge hard some ten feet from where he crouched. Cardinal hesitated a moment, eager to take a look but too disciplined to take a reckless chance that might prove his last. A rock came loose somewhere above and kicked up a clattering racket as it ricocheted off his ledge and made the big drop downwards to the spot where a frantic deputy was bawling, 'Marshal, are you all right?'

Cardinal pumped his rifle up and down overhead then started forwards still protected from above by the ledge.

Then the deputy's voice again: 'Stay put, Gene! The bastard's directly above you and if I can figure where you are then so can he.'

Cardinal studied the terrain as best he could, then started as a spray of dislodged pebbles came raining down. The deputy was right. The dry-gulcher was directly above his position, some thirty to fifty feet judging by how long it took the pebbles to drop to the ledge.

Crash!

The rifle again. This bullet struck closer but it told him something. The gunman was firing without a target. That meant he had the jitters. That was all the encouragement he needed. Cocking the rifle, he sucked in a huge breath and flung himself headlong from beneath the thrusting ledge. Landing on his right shoulder he spun onto his back and before even glimpsing a target touched off a volley of big crashing shots which echoed deafeningly loud against the rearing slabs of rock.

Then he saw him.

He was positioned between canting boulders on a ridge above and to his right by some fifty yards. He had an impression of big shoulders, a glittering

45

eye, the wicked red flare of a shot. The slug screamed off the rocks close by, but not close enough to do any more damage than pepper his shoulder with needle-like fragments of stone.

Then he was returning fire, not trying for perfect aim – not enough time for that. Just shooting fast and hoping to divert the next bullet that might come at any moment. He saw eyes glittering fiercely above a rifle barrel before he managed to get off one more shot.

A roar of rage or pain reached his ears and through the gunsmoke he saw the figure below the caprock surge to his feet and began triggering furiously. Cardinal ducked as a bullet winged past his right ear. He was sure he'd hit his man but the bastard could still throw lead. He heard Harry's shout above the uproar as he rolled then triggered twice. The figure suddenly disappeared behind the lip. Instantly Cardinal lifted his sights and sent two bullets slamming into the shadowy overhang up there.

He heard a cry.

Somehow it sounded fake.

Lightning fast, he dived beneath his stone overhang.

He was barely fast enough.

The rifle opened up like a cannon and he realized his adversary had switched positions by some hundred feet, was shooting at him from a sharper angle directly above an ancient rockslide of fragmented bluestone.

Then silence.

As the minutes dragged by he realized his shirt was plastered to his body with sweat even though the air was still cold.

He heard the sound of an empty shell being levered from a rifle. A bird hooted and somewhere a man coughed and spat.

Then, 'Gene, you all right?'

He couldn't answer. He dared not. Then Harry's voice again, suddenly excited. 'Pard, I can see the bastard!'

A rifle roared and a figure staggered into sight, tumbling off the ledge with arms and legs flailing as he plummeted through thin air. But not for long. The man hit the uppermost limits of the shale, was held up for a moment then began the slide downwards. The shale slide picked up speed and dust rose in a thick cloud. The threshing figure increased its momentum, but as gravity dragged him down past the limit of Cardinal's ledge, a powerful hand shot out, seized him by the shell belt, heaved.

Cardinal came close to being dragged onto the rushing downslide by the man's weight, but managed to stab his right toe into a crevice, then held fast. His breath burning in his lungs, he hauled the man to safety, was ready to smash an elbow into his face when he realized there was no need. He'd been struck in the shoulder and was bleeding freely.

His eyes said he was all through, so Cardinal just let him drop and stood back gasping like a grampus until his breathing returned to something like normal. By which time Harry Slater had taken a free ride down in the rockslide which had slowed to a mere trickle.

'Gene, you saved my hide,' he gasped, jumping off onto Cardinal's ledge. 'This butchering bastard tagged me out here . . . I still don't know why. . . .'

'Let's find out.'

The dazed gunman was lying propped up one one elbow now. He stared defiantly up at Cardinal, who deliberately kicked his wounded shoulder. A howl of pure agony burst from his lips and Cardinal raised his boot again, paused. 'You killed Errol Kendle, you son of a bitch. Why?'

A tear ran down the man's bloodied face. He could barely speak for the pain, but the threat hovering over him finally loosened his tongue. In silence Cardinal and Slater listened as Burke Luther, train bandit and killer, gasped out the story of how Kendle had informed on him to the law at Twin Rocks then left him to swing as he took off with the proceeds of their last big job together. It had taken Luther one week to escape, another week to track Kendle down at the ranch and gun him down.

'Only thing, Gene,' Slater broke in, 'I saw him murder Kendle, but the murdering bastard spotted me and was looking to silence me, so there was nothing left for it but to run. I was a goner when you showed, but—'

'You're still a goner, Slater,' the slowly recovering killer mouthed. His eyes flared up at Cardinal. 'You reckon I'll confess to one damn thing once they get me in a courtroom— Hey, what you got there?'

Cardinal smiled grimly as he held up the killer's pistol. It was a splendid weapon, a Remington 1861. A converted model with a loading gate and a handsome cedar butt.

'How many of these does a man see around these days?' he asked rhetorically. 'Damned few, is what. And that bullet you killed your man with is still in his body, scum. What's the betting we can't prove it came from your gun?' And they did. Burke Luther was found guilty of murder five days later in the Storytown courthouse and publicly hanged the following day.

Gene Cardinal might have been tempted to celebrate the end of a killer and the saving of his friend's life, but after just a couple of beers at the Indian Queen with Harry and his flirty wife, it was back to the routine.

From time to time Storytown might find itself light in such necessities as lamp oil, fresh drinking water and even liquor, but the big town on the plains never ran short of trouble.

CHAPTER 4

THE BIG
LONESOME

The operator of the Crawfish Creek stage depot was working on a damaged axle on his workshop lathe when he sensed a presence. Turning sharply he was startled to see a man standing in the doorway with the early sun behind him, throwing his shadow long and thin across the floor. The worker had heard nothing, the dogs had not even barked.

Unable to see the man clearly at first with the sunlight blurring his tall shape, the station boss thought momentarily of the old pistol lying behind the horse collar, but thought better of it. He'd survived ten years out here in the big lonesome by dint of hard work, diplomacy and horse sense rather than confrontation or playing the tough guy, which he wasn't anyway. So he put on a grin and said 'Howdy,' just like he was accustomed to address people showing up out of noplace with no forewarning, and without arousing the Crawfish Creek dogs.

The stranger didn't reply immediately. He was stripping black kid riding gloves from big hands and glancing about the workshed as he moved in deeper out of the early morning glare.

Suddenly the depot master could see him clearly and in that instant made his assessment. Gambling man. The stranger was around six feet tall and carried himself well in an arrogant kind of way. He wore a cutaway coat of light gray, bed of flowers vest, string tie and no hat. The face was strong and sardonic, his complexion pale yet healthy looking. Although seemingly only around thirty, his thick mane of carefully brushed-up hair was prematurely gray, the high sweep in front adding an extra couple of inches to his height.

'Howdy.' The voice was deep and impersonal. 'You the boss?'

'That's right,' the man said, setting down his clawhammer and reaching for a wad of cotton waste to swab off the sweat. 'What can I do for you, friend?' He was feeling more relaxed now that he could see that this was no hellion but plainly someone of style and quality – that's if a gambler could ever be honestly seen in such a light. He'd never cared for gambling dudes all that much, yet had never had any real trouble with the breed.

Luminous brown eyes fixed on his face. 'How's the memory?'

'What? Er, I mean, better'n average, I reckon. Why?'

'A stage en route to Storytown came through here a week ago. The manifest says there were three men and a woman on board. You recall?'

'Why, sure I do.' The man grinned, made a gesture. 'A looker like that ain't any man stuck to hell and gone out here is likely to forget in a h—'

'Describe her to me.'

The man hesitated. The stranger's voice had taken on a commanding tone. He didn't care for it. He frowned and said, 'This passenger, mister, is she kin of yours maybe?'

The stranger stared coldly.

'Are you stalling me?'

There was no longer merely a suggestion of tension; this gambling dude was riding some kind of an edge.

The depot boss wanted to hold back, fearing that in talking he might be breaching some kind of unspoken confidentiality between company and client. But the faint whiff of danger of some kind that now permeated the hushed quiet of the workshop loosened his tongue eventually.

'Like I said ... a looker. Black hair, dark eyes and style ... lots of style, if you know what I mean—'

He broke off. He was talking to himself. Hurrying to the doorway, he saw the stranger striding swiftly across the sun-washed yard towards a bay horse tied to the corral fence close by the kennels of his chained hounds.

All three dogs bared their teeth as the man swung up and rode away, yet didn't start in barking until he was out of sight along the Storytown trail.

The depot master pulled off his hat and massaged his balding head. He had a hunch that his dogs had, like himself, sensed something about the stranger which was like an unspoken warning against taking liberties, barking, talking too much, whatever.

Finally he shrugged and returned to his chores. Yet the man on the bay horse seemed to linger in his mind uneasily and for longer than he would have liked.

Ash Quentin could affect people that way, particularly when he was riled about something.

The marshal was assigning duties for the day.

He wanted two deputies posted at the railroad depot from midmorning until sundown. Three trains were due into Storytown today and he wanted a close eye kept on all new arrivals. Anyone who looked suspicious was to be checked out up front and personal, and if they failed to measure up were to be escorted to the law office where he would run the tape over them personally.

'Plain enough?'

'Yeah, Marshal, real plain.'

He then delegated the morning and afternoon street patrols to two, two-man parties, cautioning them to pay particular attention to the river docks where it was rumored certain shifty operators might attempt to bring in a shipment of smuggled guns to fuel the Indian troubles to the north.

As usual, two men were to be stationed at the

jailhouse while the remaining pair assisted over at the courthouse.

Then it was time for coffee on the jailhouse's forty-feet long front gallery with Slow Joe and the visiting V.I.P.

Major General Philip M. Sheridan of Civil War fame was about as important as any visitor could be. Young, talented, aggressive and hardheaded, this was the man who had commanded the Army of the Potomac, had shattered Jeb Stuart's gray brigades at Yellow Tavern, cleaned out the valley of the Shenandoah and finally hounded and harried Robert E Lee to surrender at Appomattox.

This was an American hero to most people including Marshal Gene Cardinal. Yet today Slow Joe Pierce found himself handling most of the conversation with the great man while his superior sipped his joe and stared off along Arkansas towards the square, his mind plainly miles away.

Luckily the soldier they called Little Phil didn't seem to notice his host's preoccupation, even made a point of thanking him for his hospitality upon leaving, even adding a little heartfelt praise.

'The Army's highly impressed with the job of work you are doing here, Marshal Cardinal. With our current problems with the tribesmen breaking loose all the way from the Arkansas to the Republican, the Cheyenne jumping their reservation at Fort Dodge and Comanches and Kiowas causing their usual ructions in the valleys of the Saline and the Solomon, it's damned reassuring to know that in Storytown we have a rock solid supply and transportation center not vulnerable to local upheavals and lawlessness. It was not always so, as you well know, and the very welcome change is, I know, correctly attributable to you. Keep up the good work, sir.'

The two men shook, saluted, and Sheridan was off with his glittering retinue to go clattering across Republic Square – a deliberate and timely reminder to the city that behind the law forces of this and every place like it lay the might of Uncle Sam's armed forces.

This was always a boost for the lawmen of the day, and Slow Joe Pierce for one was highly appreciative. How his superior felt there was no telling. Cardinal was acting like he was miles away today and the first deputy reckoned he knew why.

'Nice feller, the general, Gene.'

No answer.

'I figured he'd be different. You know? Meaner and ornerier. I guess it's true what they say. Most people are like a bob-wire fence. They all have their good points.'

'Hmm. . . .'

'OK,' Slow Joe said, 'I give up trying to be funny. You claim you don't want to talk about it but the way you act says the opposite. What do you aim to do about Miss Winters?'

Cardinal rose to toss coffee grounds over the porch railing. 'Haven't you heard?' he said, poker faced. 'I'm deporting her back to Dodge, closing down the Palace and serving papers on Branco for unloading a property on someone the law office doesn't rightly approve of.'

For a moment Pierce almost swallowed it. Then he realized he was being had. He was not amused.

'Of course if you want to clown around when a man wants to discuss something this serious, then you can go to—'

'Relax, man,' Cardinal said soberly, taking his hat from the rack. 'The reason we don't talk about Rebecca is there's simply nothing much of anything to talk about. She's here and that's that.'

'But it's getting under your skin.'

'Lots of things do that.'

'You could force her out, man.'

'I believe I'm quoting you correctly when I say – never try to run a bluff when your poke's empty.'

'Does that mean you can't or won't?'

'Both, if you like.'

Slow Joe moved to the top of the steps as Cardinal descended, his expression blank yet somehow taut.

'This whole thing is not doing you one lick of good, Gene. Seems everybody and his dog knows all about you and this woman and how she dumped you for another man down south. Even I don't know if that's true or not, but that doesn't much matter. You're giving your enemies something to feed on and make cheap jokes about. "Hey, did you hear about the town tamer who couldn't tame his own woman?" That sort of guff. It's no secret that your standing as tall as you do here is the single most important factor in this here office keeping the lid on Storytown. But this sort of thing could chip away at your standing, and who knows where that might lead?'

'You worry too much.'

'OK, I know what you're saying. "Back off, Slow Joe". So, where are you off to now?'

'Council meeting, coffee with the railroad engineers about the new spur . . . the regular stuff. You mind the shop.'

'Don't I always?'

'And you do a good job.'

'Don't soft soap me, Gene. I'm too old for that. Walk careful.'

'You too.'

Maybe the deputy's warning was responsible for the marshal's change of plans that day, or maybe that had been lurking in the back of his mind anyway. Whatever the case, he promptly cancelled his scheduled meetings and did what he often did as marshal of Storytown. He took himself for a long walk around the big sprawling town which most people claimed he had successfully tamed single-handed, which might well be the case.

Might.

Cardinal never claimed victory until certain that the fat lady had well and truly sung her song. Past experience had taught him that towns, like people, had a nasty way of striking back at you when least expected, just when you were ready to count them out.

Deep down he knew he was more than satisfied with the results his admittedly harsh rule had had here, and there was every indication that law and order would continue to prevail.

But this town was different from other places he'd tamed in his time insofar as the overtly wild and criminal element was not the only or even the most formidable foe he was called upon to deal with.

Here, it was the wheelers and dealers you had to watch. Big operators like Branco who wanted a wide-open, anything-goes kind of city which would continue to attract commerce and cash for operators such as himself to skim off any which way they might, legally or the other way.

Men like Branco rarely challenged men in his position openly, but were inclined to do so covertly which made them all the more dangerous.

But today Gene Cardinal wasn't concerned with such men or even the problems they generated as he set out. He would do what he did every so often in order not to lose touch with the real heartbeat of the city. He would make the rounds, not of the plush hotels and saloons, nor the board rooms or the office of the mayor, the chambers of the judges or the rarefied atmosphere of the Plains Cattlemen's Association or the places where the movers and shakers hung their hats. Instead he meant to tune into the sounds, smells, voices, music and simple feel of the city's underbelly in order that he might do his job better.

His way led down Dixie where the elevated tracks of the Grand West Railroad walked across several blocks on criss-crossed trellises which cast patterns of shadow across the dusty streets.

From there his steps led him down to the river, back across to Circle Street then along the long stone wall of the abattoirs and on to slumtown with its half-naked kids, its shadowy bars and brazen prostitutes who called out ribald propositions to him that almost made him smile.

He'd stopped for a cold beer at a riverside joint when Harry Slater found him.

The rancher was in town on business but had sighted him heading for Circle Street and realized he too was thirsty.

'Cheers, Gene.'

'Looking at you, Harry.'

The rancher lowered his tankard. 'I heard about it.'

Cardinal nodded. He knew what the man meant.

'Nothing to fuss about, Harry.'

'Want to talk about it?'

'Nope.'

Harry grinned broadly. 'Thank God for that! If there's any joker in the Territory worse at discussing women, analyzing women or even satisfying women, I'd have to meet him before I could believe it.'

Cardinal studied the rancher. Slater had been through a rough spell but looked just like his old self, off-beat, quick-moving, a jittery bright-eyed eccentric with a talent for trouble but an even greater one for friendship.

The marshal didn't boast many friends, and he knew it disturbed a lot of people that his closest friend here was what many considered to be a borderline nutter. They were, of course, wrong about that.

'How's the wife, Harry?'

The rancher sobered and fingered his goatee. 'Still playing the good woman – since the killing, I mean.'

'Women, eh?'

'Well, seeing as you brought up the subject—'

'It's all over, man,' Cardinal cut him off, gazing out over the batwings. 'I'm not sure why she's here or why she bought the old French Palace, but I'd be double puzzled if it had anything to do with me. Another?'

They had one more and the cattleman was on his way, riding off along the ramshackle street and whistling like a man without a care in the world, which maybe was the case.

Cardinal smiled after him but was sober again as he donned his Stetson and stepped down into the dust to continue his patrol.

At times like this he reminded himself he should socialize more and obsess about law and order less.

He had always been a serious and often relentless man of the law and more so since taking over here, he had to admit.

Even so, by mid afternoon with several hours of patrolling and yarning and stopping off for the added occasional beer he was feeling damned good infinitely better and more relaxed than when he'd set out.

At last the entire Lazy X affair was beginning to

fade from his mind. No matter how often you were called on to gun a man down, it never got to feel right.

But knowing he'd saved an innocent man from the gallows helped ease his mind.

There were hours of sunlight left yet and he knew he could visit the depot, the poolrooms, the up-a-flight gambling dens and the basement drug holes down by the Key. He had the energy, was attuned to the pulsebeat he was looking for and felt all the better for slogging it out on sunbaked streets rather than consulting with men wearing fifty-dollar silk shirts. Or, worse still, putting in an obligatory appearance at one of the mayor's wife's afternoon parties at which, for some perverse reason, the good lady and her society sisters often absolutely insisted he attend.

In truth he might end up anyplace in Storytown, but one. There was no way the marshal would be stopping by the renamed Rosetta Saloon. Not today, likely not any day.

And the people he talked with, the washer-women and cheap drunks, the levee men and the cowhands loading stock at the depot – all seemed to convey the same encouraging impression that long afternoon. Seemed to him, that although curious regarding the stories circulating about him and Rebecca Winters, the man in the street couldn't care less what had happened in his past, providing it didn't affect the way he maintained law and order here, protected their interests and kept the city on the plains a safer place to live.

He was back at the docks watching the loading of lumber aboard a paddle wheel freighter at sunset at the same time a lone rider came in off the plains from the south on a long-legged bay horse.

CHAPTER 5

DEAL ME IN

It was early the following evening and Emil Branco was growing testy.

'Look, you hicks,' he said, hunching meaty shoulders and interlocking stubby fingers as he leaned forward in his chair over his desk. 'It's time we got something straight. This is my deal, I make the decisions and all you sodbusters have gotta do is be patient, cool your heels and just wait for your big pay day. So, that being the case, what in hell are you doing in town using up my valuable time?'

The spacious office at the back of the Mogul was thick with tobacco smoke and simmering hostility.

Either sitting awkwardly or standing uneasily before that outsized black mahogany desk where so many of the city's big deals were hatched, was a cluster of sun-darkened men in overalls and straw hats. They grandiosely titled themselves the Bow

Creek Farmers' Association, but were more gener-
ally known as 'them sodbusters holdin' up the
Grand West Railroad's spur line to Cottonfield.'

The wizened leader drew a curved briar from
yellowed teeth and spoke in a twang like a badly
tuned banjo.

'And jist how long are we supposed to wait, Mr
Branco?'

'Until I say it's time to squeeze the last dollar out
of that tight-fisted railroad, is what,' came the curt
reply.

'They's talk thet the Grand West might be losin'
interest in their spur,' chimed in another.
'Where'll we all be iffen they pull out?'

Branco reached for a jug of beer and poured
himself another. None for anybody else. These
hicks were really riling him. Several months earlier
when he'd first gotten wind of the railroad's plans
for the spur, he had promptly hatched up his plan
to block the line by uniting the sodbusters under
his banner and holding out for the biggest possible
price – for the farmers and himself as agent. The
miserable plough-pushers had been happy enough
to go along with him – until the railroad fired up
the scary rumor that they might scrap the whole
plan if they didn't immediately get their way at the
price they were prepared to pay for their right-of-
way: not what the farmers were holding out for.

Now they were knocking his door down to tell
him they were scared, insisting he sell while the
selling was still on.

Sell, hell!

That was his attitude. But he sensed they thought they might get one over him now simply because they owned the crummy dirt the railroad wanted to cross, while he was – as one had actually referred to him earlier – simply their business adviser.

The ungrateful sons of bitches!

Yet in the same breath he found himself cautioning himself not to risk it all by blowing his top.

'Boys, boys—' he began placatingly as he rose, but ragged-assed Hick Donovan had the gall to speak over him.

'We ain't boys, yours or anybody else's, Branco,' the man declared righteously. 'Fellers, are we gonna let him try and talk us out of what he knows we gotta do, or are we gonna stand together and agree to do a deal while the deal's still in the offin'? And just in case any of you might be wonderin' howcome it's all kinda urgent with me, I'm three months in arrears on my lousy land rates right as I'm standing here.'

That hit home.

When Branco saw that even the stronger ones were beginning to look like waverers he suddenly reached a decision. Crash through or crash. That precept for handling business ventures had worked for him often enough before – worth another try here.

'And where would you be if you took that course? Might I take it on the chin . . . or might you geezers start being picked out of the deeps at Breakneck Bend with weights attached? C'mon, do you get the picture or are you even too hick-dumb to do that?'

The moment the words were out, Branco regretted them. But not for long, for at that moment, having been listening from the saloonkeeper's washroom in back, big Sy Clanton abruptly entered the room.

Everyone stopped talking.

Branco's chief bouncer was a dangerous man and looked it, every inch.

The ranchers were struck silent as the heavyweight took up a position before the black desk. 'You was saying, boss?'

From that point on it proved relatively easy for Branco to dominate his audience and have them touching their forelocks before Clanton saw them off.

It was a triumph of sorts yet the big man was slumped deep in his chair with more furrows in his brow than a forty-acre back lot by the time the bouncer returned.

'Hey, what's the matter, boss man? They knuckled under and they ain't gonna be back for quite a spell, I reckon. So what's the gripe?'

Branco bit off an inch of a fresh golden Cuban and spat it halfway across the room. Clanton struck a vesta and lighted him up. He wasn't thanked for it.

'Bitching sodbusters, griping bankers, crooked dealers and . . . and who . . . who really gives a rat's ass about his damned tart showing up any longer anyway . . . that's what I want to know. . . ?'

The big man pricked his ears. 'We're talking about Cardinal now, boss man?'

'I figured to get enough mileage out of that ex-dame of Cardinal's showing up to prick that tinstar's bubble for good and maybe even get to see him off. I even gave her a special deal on the price for the Palace to make sure she stayed on here to make her job of getting him back all that easier . . . if that's what she's here for. . . .'

He paused to belch smoke at the ceiling.

'But what happens? Sure, we had a few good days of whispering and sniggering and hot gossip. But all the time Cardinal walks around as though he doesn't give a rap, she won't even talk about him to nobody nohow, so now it's like it's all yesterday's news and who gives a shit anyway? That tinstar must be gold-plated the way things work out for him.'

Clanton rested a ham on the desk corner and admired his axle-oil coiffure in a glassed print. He liked what he saw but was suitably sympathetic to his boss.

'I guess it was too much to ask that we mighta got shook of him that easy.'

Clanton massaged a bull jaw that still seemed to ache from a pistol whipping the marshal had handed him when he elected to take the lawman on.

He hadn't tried it since.

'I guess there's one thing positive about all this,' Branco sighed at last. 'At least all that Dodge City gossip and suchlike has cut the marshal down some . . . and so far it seems he hasn't any suspicion that it's me what's holding up the Grand West's plans here.'

Now he sat erect. 'Pour me a shot and get back to the tables, Sy. I'll depress myself if I keep up this kind of talk.'

He was well into a pile of paperwork by lamplight when his man reappeared an hour later.

'What?' he grouched without looking up.

'We got a geezer interested in the faro dealer's job, boss.'

'What's he shape up like?'

'Looks the part. Dealt a couple of hands like a real pro. Could be kind of uppity though.'

'I fired the last dealer on that count. Tell him no.'

It wasn't long before Clanton was back. 'He says he wants to talk to you personal, boss. Matter of fact he says he insists. That was how he put it.'

'God's teeth!' the saloonkeeper yelled, screwing up a sheet of paper and hurling it at the wall. 'I'm trying to get stuff done here. He doesn't get the job, and nobody insists with me. Throw him out.'

He was skilfully tallying rows of figures a short time later when above the murmur of voices, music and clinking glassware he heard someone shout. This was followed by a crash and a scream.

He rose and strode through the outer room to the bar where he glimpsed some kind of altercation taking place in the keno room. As he shouldered his way through the mob he saw one of his dealers groggily hanging on to a heavy drape with one hand and nursing a bloodied mouth with the other. The drop lamps gleamed upon a husky stranger with silver hair standing with fists cocked and challenging all comers.

The man might have stepped from a glossy magazine illustration of the classic Western gambling man. Added to that he appeared fearless and totally sure of himself, and suddenly Emil Branco suspected he was looking at the mysterious job applicant he'd just been told of.

Just going by appearances, he thought the fellow appeared likely enough. But he must be tested out first.

He whistled shrilly through his teeth and immediately the Mogul's muscle converged on the keno room in double quick time. A bloody-faced Clanton heaved himself away from the side curtains to lead the combined assault upon the stranger. It was a mistake. The newcomer glimpsed trouble coming from the corner of his eye. He whirled like a boxer and delivered a perfectly timed smash to the point of the jaw which drove Clanton clear through the curtained window and into the street.

Branco was astonished, his bruisers hesitant. Clanton was his best man by a street length.

The stranger jabbed a finger at him.

'Look, fatso,' he panted, 'I still want this job and I'm the best freaking dealer you're going to meet this year. So why the hooraw?'

'I . . . I. . . .' gasped Branco, a dangerous man, but too far removed from actual violence by money and security to be physically effective any longer. But in that moment his security was regrouping and moving in at strength. Tall Murdock clamped a lightning headlock on the troublemaker from behind while another hurled a blow that missed. The stranger drove a pistoning elbow into Murdock's guts and the man reeled away, bent double and puking.

A full scale brawl was raging when the batwings burst open and Marshal Cardinal came striding in.

'Next man that moves is under arrest. Branco, didn't I warn you about—'

He broke off abruptly. Slowly the brawl petered out. They were waiting for the marshal to continue but Cardinal was staring fixedly at the silver-haired newcomer.

'Quentin!'

The Mogul crowd was initially slow to react to that name, yet react they eventually did. They'd heard it before. Often. It was likely that the fat man's eyes bugged widest of all as a ripple of surprise ran through the crowd surrounding him.

'Quentin?' he croaked, leaning towards the stranger. 'You're him? Ash Quentin, isn't it?'

'What if it is, lard guts?'

The newcomer was focused on the badgeman as he thrust his way through the onlookers. He ran fingers through his hair, his chest rising and falling from exertion and a thin trickle of blood running from the corner of his mouth.

Then he said tonelessly, 'Cardinal. Been a time.'

'Who is responsible for this ruckus?'

The marshal's calm brought groans of disappointment from drinkers anticipating fireworks. For the story concerning their marshal, Rebecca Winters and a man named Quentin up in Dodge was widely circulated. They expected fireworks, not calm.

'He is!'

Quentin and Branco spoke together, pointing fingers at each other. But then, paradoxically Branco suddenly grinned and clapped a hand to Quentin's shoulder.

'Hey, what am I saying? I'm not a man to hold a grudge. Let bygones be bygones is my motto, Quentin. We just got off on the wrong foot, is all. You still want that job?' He smirked at the marshal. 'Or maybe you'd rather try your luck down at the new-named Rosetta on Dixie Street, huh? You were lucky with that new boss lady up in Dodge so I hear tell. Like, real lucky?'

Quentin pivoted smoothly from the hips to chop a brutal, close-range punch into the saloon-keeper's fat mouth. Crimson flew and Emil Branco smacked the floor and rolled several feet until halted against the legs of the astonished onlookers.

Quentin was lunging after his man when a quiet voice halted him. 'That's enough, Quentin!' said Cardinal, and the gambler halted, fists still bunched, eyes holding a cold clear shine.

'He asked for it, Cardinal.'

'I'm not denying that.'

It seemed only too plain to all now that Rebecca Winters must be a touchy topic with the newcomer gambling man. This led the onlookers to surmise that maybe all that local gossip concerning the Dodge City love triangle might hold some validity after all.

Yet if this were the case, then how come Marshal Cardinal appeared so calm and detached?

'No more trouble here tonight,' was all he said, and left them standing in silence listening to the sound of his boot-heels on the plankwalk outside fade away into stillness.

Everyone turned to stare speculatively at Ash Quentin whose handsome features now showed nothing at all.

'How many times have you been arrested, Browny?'

'Why, every time I gets out of jail, Deputy sir.'

'Well, you're getting back in, right now. Next!'

Slow Joe Pierce's tired eyes studied the next and final reprobate to be presented before him under that revealing drop light, a stringbean youth with a knife-scarred face and red-rimmed bloodhound eyes.

'You don't have to tell me your name, son,' he sighed. 'I know it, but I never use bad language. You're charged with chopping off a John's finger while working as a pimp at Lucy Carol's. How do you plead?'

'Never used a blade in my life, Deputy,' insisted this knife-hacked wreck. 'And I was workin' at Lucy's as a dancer.'

'Keep an eye on him or he might waltz right out

of here under our noses. Take him down.'

And it was over for another night. The spectators filed out, the lights were extinguished and Slow Joe and three deputies quit the show-up room to walk the short distance to the law office, where hot coffee and biscuits were waiting.

'Where was the marshal tonight, does anyone know?' Pierce inquired wearily as he perched on a corner of Cardinal's long desk.

'Who knows?' a freckle-faced deputy replied, glancing at his companions. 'Marshal Cardinal was always pretty reliable once but somehow doesn't quite seem that way any more.'

Slow Joe studied them over the rim of his coffee mug. The deputies' eyes were full of questions. They were all of them aware of the change that had come over Cardinal since the arrival of the new owner of the former French Palace. And of course they couldn't help but pick up on those stories linking Cardinal with Rebecca Winters and Ash Quentin, but nothing more. Their silence seemed to be telling Pierce that they felt it was time they knew more, and he supposed this was so.

'Wiseacres still making cracks?' he asked.

Heads nodded.

'Happens all the time, Slow Joe. Guess it's not doin' any of us much good havin' to listen to people take digs at the marshal and us not knowin' how to hit back,' said the youngest deputy on the payroll, a tough, husky youth of just twenty.

'Well, reckon I don't want any hitting back,' Pierce sighed, lowering his mug. 'But I guess you ought to know. . . . So listen up and you'll get it straight just once. . . .'

He made the story of Marshal Cardinal and Rebecca Winters accurate, or at least as accurate as any outsider could.

He paused, contemplating the past before continuing.

'Then along came Quentin. I can't tell you when he and Miss Winters got started or when Gene found out about them. It hit him pretty hard. But he took it on the chin, like you'd expect.' A shrug. 'So he quit Dodge and took over here, and like always I tagged along after him. End of story.'

'That's it?' queried one.

'Just up and quit?' another asked disbelievingly. 'The marshal didn't haul this Quentin out behind the barn and kick the crap out of him?'

'Nothing like that.' Pierce told them. 'Maybe he thought of it, I wouldn't know. Then again, it could have been a bad idea even if he'd considered it.'

'Huh?' the husky youth said. 'What do you mean, Slow Joe?'

Pierce eyed the man levelly. 'Quentin is a killer.'

The deputies stared.

Then, 'He ain't on the files as such, Deputy,' said one, 'on account I took the trouble to look.'

'That's right, he ain't,' Pierce affirmed, sliding off the desk to stand in the doorway, looking out. 'When he kills, he does it fair and square. He's a duellist, and he's put more than one man in his grave. So now you know enough both to treat him

74

wary and keep a close eye on him. I don't know what brought him here this way but I've a powerful hunch it's not for anything good.'

'It'd have to have something to do with that purty woman though, wouldn't it, Slow Joe?' the husky deputy asked with a frown. 'Ain't that plain?'

'Maybe not,' Pierce said in a way that indicated he was tiring of the subject. 'Guess I forgot to tell you that I heard a whisper a couple of weeks back that Quentin and Miss Winters had broke up.' He shrugged. 'Of course it just could be that the man's come here with a mind to try and win her back. What would I know?'

'What does the marshal reckon about all this?' he was asked.

'That's the worrying part,' he replied quietly, reaching for his pipe. 'Gene's saying nothing at all. And that just ain't natural.'

The hand-written note read:

Gene,
Please meet me at the new corral in back of the saloon at five to discuss an important matter.
Rebecca

He sat for a long minute tapping the envelope against his thumb before getting up and drawing on his waist jacket. He supposed he was pleased she had contacted him – he had been avoiding her and the saloon up until now. Maybe it might have continued on that way but for Ash Quentin showing in town. Plainly that was something neither of them could afford to overlook.

He walked outside, across Main then down Pipeclay Alley. The evening was already cold and he passed a cluster of bare-legged kids crouched round a pine-cone fire, trying to heat up a can of something or other.

He sighted her straightaway in the gloom upon reaching the corral. She was seated on a bale of straw, wearing a tailored suit of some soft material, a brightly colored neckerchief. Her face lighted up when she saw him and she came rushing toward him with outstretched arms, then halted as though to compose herself, which was unusual. Unusual because Rebecca was always composed.

'I'm so glad you came,' she said evenly. 'It's nice to see you again, Gene.'

'Likewise.' He paused, waiting for the expected kick to the heart. It didn't come. He stood before the corral railings and added,'You look fine, but then you always did. New business going well?'

'We're not here to talk business, Gene.'

'Guess not. Quentin?' he guessed.

She nodded and began pacing up and down before him, drawing her shawl about her shoulders. She was as beautiful as ever, he couldn't help noting.

'I was as shocked as you must have been when he showed. I thought it was all over between us, I thought I'd made that plain to him in Dodge.'

'It was you who broke it off then?'

'Of course.' Her tone told him she found that a

76

strange question. And he supposed it was. It was certainly she who had ended their affair. He'd been as much in love with her that day as he had been at the start when she calmly told him there was somebody else. Quentin.

She ceased pacing and stood before him, the wind teasing her hair.

'It just didn't work out with Ash. I won't go into why. Suffice to say I'd had enough and told him so.'

'He doesn't strike as a man who'd take something like that lying down. Did he?'

'At first he seemed all right.'

'At first?'

She nodded. 'Then I sold up and came here that same week.'

'Why here?'

He was impressed by how calm he sounded. It was not how he'd expected to be.

'I needed to see you,' came the unhesitant reply.

'Why, Rebecca?'

'I can't explain why . . . at least not yet. But I was prepared to wait and see what happened, to sort out my feelings.' A slight pause. 'You see, Gene, I realized I might have made a huge mistake leaving you, and wanted to. . . . Well, never mind that now. I came here, I settled in, I was glad I'd done it. And then he appeared. . . .'

'He wants you back?' She nodded and he went on. 'Where do I come into all this?'

She lifted her chin. 'I'm sure I don't know. I only know Ash was enraged when he learned I was coming here. He's been acting calm and normal when he's visited the saloon. But I know him too well. He's anything but normal underneath.' Now she stepped forward and placed her palms on his chest, looking up at him with those deathless black eyes. 'I'm afraid of what he's thinking, what he might do. Honestly, Gene, I simply wanted to get away to someplace quiet and distant and gather myself together. I never imagined he would follow me, or threaten you. . . .'

'He's made threats?'

'Of course. And not just against you, both of us—'

She broke off at the sound of hurried steps. Cardinal's hand dropped to his gunbutt, then took it off when Slow Joe's runty form emerged from the dusky gloom. The deputy tugged off his five-gallon and nodded at Rebecca before turning to Cardinal.

'Sorry to interrupt, Marshal, but the Jacksons are at it again . . . along by the depot they are. Got a real ruckus going, so they have.'

'I'll have to go,' he said to her. He half grinned. 'Duty still. Deputy, escort Miss Rebecca back.' He touched his hatbrim. 'I'll consider what you told me and we'll talk again.'

He was still puzzled how calm and uninvolved he felt as he set out for the depot. But he was anything but detached upon arriving at the depot to find a freight train at the station and a wild brawl spilling over the railroad tracks down by the ticket office.

The Jacksons were normally four easy-going

brothers but for when they were drinking and they mostly were drinking. He'd clashed with them before and the moment long haired Mike Jackson sighted him coming towards them he lowered his rum-addled head and charged.

The man ran head-on into a chopping blow from a sixgun barrel. He struck earth so hard he bounced. Cardinal stepped over him and kicked Billy Jackson's feet from beneath him before his sixgun butt made violent contact with Joey Jackson's buck teeth.

Blood sprayed and the marshal winced as Nigel Jackson broke a cattle prod across his back that sent him staggering several yards before regaining his balance. He whirled and headbutted the charging cowboy with an impact that sent both men staggering backwards.

A figure loomed before his dazed eyes and he let fly with with a truly brutal right hook that knocked the man to his knees, spitting crimson.

It was all over that quick and soon the deputies showed up to haul the brothers off to the lockup.

For a time Cardinal stood sucking his knuckles and watching them go. He still didn't feel much of anything other than maybe a little sore across the back. Maybe he'd react differently to the dramatic meeting with Rebecca back at the corral after he had these wild men under lock and key.

Maybe.

CHAPTER 6

THE TORCH STILL BURNS

Cardinal quit the diner and walked into the echoing street. He halted at the corner of Walnut and West to touch a vesta to his cheroot. His gaze was reflective as he drew deeply. The misting night was close, muffling sound. As always, his ears were pricked for trouble while on this occasion his mind was far away.

From somewhere near Lower Dixie Street, in the direction of the river, came the sound of a muffled crash, like that of a rig rolling over or maybe some roisterer overturning a stumble-bum's lean-to, he mused. That was the rough end of the city and there was always some kind of trouble on the simmer down there. Mostly the law didn't interfere unless there was actual bloodshed or the threat of it. Lower Dixie Streeters had a way of sorting things out amongst themselves mostly, which suited the marshal just fine. He liked to concentrate his forces up here in the central half-dozen big blocks where the movers and shakers, the lawful and lawless, all plied their trade.

A hulking figure encased in a dirty gray Mackinaw tramped by on the plankwalk, a grudging, 'Marshal,' coming from the unkempt figure.

Cardinal nodded. Respect was what it was all about, and he got it. Reluctant or otherwise, he didn't care which just so long as it was forthcoming. Of course, of late there had been a drop off in the high level of popularity he'd come to expect, due largely to the witch's cauldron of gossip whipped up by the arrival of Rebecca and Quentin.

Kids scrawled things on walls and you might catch the odd offensive remark shouted from a crowd or under cover of darkness, but overall it did not amount to much. Nobody dared taunt him face to face in Storytown. If they should, they would wind up in cuffs and behind bars in that order, sure as sunrise. That was how he ran trouble towns, new saloonkeepers or gambling house dealers notwithstanding.

He moved on.

Two horsemen came along the glistening street, hunched in their saddles and swinging bottles from their hands. Riders from the Running D heading home after a blow-out. In a cross street he glimpsed the rear end of a wagon laden with buffalo hides disappearing toward the rail depot.

Some ambitious teamster working crazy hours to buy his stake in the Golden West, no doubt.

The marshal liked Storytown best of all the places where he'd worn the five-pointed star. This was because it was both the biggest and had responded best to his particular brand of law enforcement. In Storytown an honest man could envisage the future, solid, prosperous and lawful. Of course the sprawling regional center would only achieve its full potential if the men who wore the stars maintained their edge over those who would take over and run things in their fashion, if you let them.

Until just recently the city marshal had been totally focused on maintaining this hard-won status quo. Yet he was well aware tonight that, as had been the case for nigh on two weeks now, both his concentration and commitment to the job were way down.

He still put in the hours, was just as quick as ever with a word, a clip in the ear or a sixgun rammed into the ribs when necessary. But at most times there was the uneasy feeling that, while discharging the familiar rituals and duties his head was someplace else altogether.

His wandering steps had led him away from Walnut and down along Dixie to the halfway point which was marked by the two-storied, high-fronted and slightly gaudy façade of the Rosetta saloon.

The building's lights were blurred by the rain yet he could see enough through the windows to know there was still a sizable crowd even at this late hour.

Nothing surprising in that. Rebecca always ran a good place. And even if a large percentage of the drinkers to be found on her premises at any given time happened to be at least halfway in love with her, then what harm was there in that if they kept the cash register ticking over?

Better than anyone, he knew what it was like to love her.

'A crush, Marshal?' he asked aloud, lips twisting down at the corners. Of course it had been more than that. Much more.

But he knew that regret was a far cry from being in love.

Their break-up over her involvement with Ash Quentin had been painful. But on the positive side it had also been quick, clean and final. He always knew he'd done the sensible thing in quitting Dodge and setting up here, fully expecting never to see her again.

Her arrival in Storytown had been a shock, a genuine bolt from the blue. He did not swallow her story about simply running a market check when looking around to set up a new place, and Storytown just happened to be the place that met all her commercial requirements.

No matter how often he pondered on that, it still didn't wash.

She'd fallen in love with someone else in Dodge, as any woman had a right to do. But travelling a hundred miles to set up shop in his town? Knowing her as well as he did, he sensed some kind of ruthless decision-making in that big move.

But why?

What could be the motive?

And where the hell did Quentin fit in?

One thing was for sure. Although Quentin appeared intent on maintaining the idea that he just 'happened' to show in Storytown, Cardinal didn't swallow one word of it.

Nor did Rebecca. He was certain of that also. But neither of them was easy to read when they put the shutters up. He'd never had even a hint that Rebecca had fallen for someone else in Dodge until the day she told him so.

That had been on a Friday. Black Friday he called it. His worst day. But he'd survived it.

He frowned at a thought. Maybe he was flattering himself, but from the day of their meeting at the corral he'd had the clear impression she was playing up to him. Since then there had been the invitations to supper which he hadn't accepted. Sometimes she stopped by at the jailhouse when she was out 'shopping.' With little gifts.

Somehow he felt all that might have been unsettling enough even without Quentin showing.

First her, then her ex-lover . . . that's if he really was 'ex'.

What sort of sense did it all make?

That was how his thinking was running at that moment, standing across the street from the Rosetta in the rain. He was a deeply puzzled and suspicious man in that moment, when it happened.

The muffled sound of a single shot sounding

from the direction of the river could not have come at a better time. In a moment, the marshal of Storytown was on his way. Within the hour a drink-addled ferryman who'd touched off a shot just to liven things up, found himself behind bars for the night suffering double vision from a pistol whipping and nursing his lumps, wondering what the Sam Hill he had done to make the marshal so touchy.

Ash Quentin sat in the porch shade of the Federal Hotel with a fragrant cigar dangling from his teeth looking vaguely amused by the interest he still commanded at the end of his second week in the city. He appeared debonair and relaxed in an immaculately tailored suit of gray broadcloth, was aware of the interest of two pretty shopgirls walking by but didn't bother smiling, didn't need to where females were concerned. They remained interested anyway. There'd been a time when he might have responded to any pretty woman and shown her a high old time. Not here though. Not in Storytown. Everything was different in Storytown, for he'd never been to anyplace for the dark reasons that had brought him here.

His Stetson hat sat on the small table before him alongside a deck of cards.

He brushed his right hand over his silver thatch in a habitual gesture then reached out and picked up the playing cards.

Automatically he began to cut and sort the pasteboards by suit and number. After that, he quickly cut, recut and shuffled again.

He frowned at the result. For some reason the cards weren't behaving the way they should. Did that mean he wasn't really concentrating?

Maybe so.

He boxed the deck and leaned back, replacing his hat to cut down the glare.

There was an increasing bustle of mid morning activity along the street already, with horsemen and people afoot going about their business.

He'd often been told that whenever he was around people had a feeling something was going to happen.

If they were thinking that in Storytown, Sloane County, they might well be proven right before he was through.

As he leant forward to ash his cheroot in a brass spittoon by the chair, his money belt dug into his flesh. He was smiling again as he leaned back. Branco paid him well above top dollar to deal, and he had managed to take a few high rollers for big bucks at poker and blackjack at rival establishments in his spare time.

Life in Storytown was good but he knew it wouldn't last.

All his life Quentin had displayed a talent for converting respect and admiration into fear and hate. It was his nature and his twisted pleasure.

A sneer rode his mouth. He might laugh in public to overhear himself being labeled a fast gun, a son of a bitch, and far worse. He took pride in that. But on this journey to this town there was pain and rage that nobody knew of ; they only perceived his arrogance and vanity.

His thoughts turned inward and his cigar burned away unnoticed. . . .

They'd first met on the fabled streets of Dodge City the very day he came to town looking to kill a man.

She was tending Gene Cardinal who'd been wounded in a shootout with a lone rider linked to the James Gang. The two had been together half a year when she quit the four-bed hospital and came face to face with the most handsome man she'd ever met.

Quentin knew how to play on his charm and good looks and within a week she was sharing his accommodation at the Great West Hotel and a rejected Cardinal was responding to a job offer from Storytown Council to come and clean up their county as City Marshal.

Sometime during the idyllic months together that followed for Ash Quentin and Rebecca Winters, the impossible happened. The gambler with the lightning draw and uncertain temper fell in love, something that had never happened during all his years of philandering and gunslinging.

She told him she loved him in return, but he was never totally sure. Even so, he knew he believed it was for keeps right up until the unforgettable day some months later when he returned to their suite at the hotel to discover she'd moved back to the hotel she ran on Beale Street.

She left him a farewell letter. It was over. Just like that.

Accepting defeat well was a skill he'd never mastered, whether it be at the hands of gunmen or women, and when he realized she was not coming back the threats began. He would give her a month to relent, otherwise. . . . He didn't fill in the blanks, didn't have to. He was plainly a man obsessed and knew his towering vanity would never allow him to be publicly humiliated by either another man of the gun or a woman.

Then, overnight she quit Dodge and travelled to Storytown where Cardinal bossed the streets. Apparently, jealousy joined hands with rejection for Quentin at that point, and he was soon heading for Storytown with retribution on his mind.

It seemed possible that a murderously enraged Quentin might well have put both his former lover and the marshal in their graves by this time, but for the fact that there was no outward sign that Cardinal was even vaguely interested in his former mistress now.

Quentin's sick rage was salved by this. But it still simmered even if expertly concealed. For curiosity and jealousy demanded he find out for certain that she had fled to the marshal's arms before he acted. He had to know the truth.

He'd attempted to approach Cardinal without success; the marshal chose who he socialized with and the gunman was not on his list. Strangely enough, Rebecca had been more forthcoming in their only meeting thus far. She'd had either the courage or foolishness to admit she had come to Storytown upon realizing she was still in love with her former lawman lover.

He'd considered going after the marshal that very night, but something stayed his hand. One admission didn't represent proof. He needed to know – perhaps even catch them together – in order to believe the worst. Then would come the vengeance with a thunder of gunshots.

By now a large part of the rage he'd first directed solely towards his former lover had become centered on the man he believed was trying to steal her back. . . .

He came back to the present with a jolt.

A woman emerged from the hotel entrance opposite, tall, stately and plainly affluent. Unfurling her umbrella before venturing out into the weak sun, she glanced his way. He expected her to sail off with her nose in the air. Instead she crossed the street toward him in her immaculate French shoes with button straps and tiny flowers sewn into the stitching.

'You're Mr Quentin, aren't you?'

'I am. But you have the advantage of me, Ma'am.' He didn't rise. He was only mannerly when it suited .

'I'm Carlotta Roebuck.'

'You are a handsome woman, Carlotta.'

She flushed a little at the compliment.

'May I ask you a question, sir?'

'That's what I'm here for – just lazing away my time waiting for the pretty ladies in town to sashay by and start asking me questions. If you want to start off by inquiring if I'm an expert on good-looking women, sex, then the answer's an unequivocal yes.'

His teeth showed in a fixed smile. He was aware of the effect he could have on women but saw that Carlotta Roebuck was obviously determined not to be diverted from the business at hand.

'Can you tell me if your coming to Storytown is meant in some way to discommode Marshal Cardinal, sir?'

'Discommode? Why, bless my soul, do I look like a fellow who would discommode anyone, fair lady? Much less a man as big and important as your m—'

'If you have come to cause Gene Cardinal trouble of some kind,' she cut in brusquely, 'then I should advise you that he has the support of every decent and law abiding citizen in this city. And in case you are wondering, ninety percent of Storytown's city's rich and powerful – business-men, judges, the wealthy and the influential – are happy to classify themselves as supporters of the law office, one hundred percent. Am I making myself clear, sir?'

'If you are warning me to watch my step and not tread on Gene's toes, you got me straight between the eyes. Bullseye. But seeing I'm being honest with you, will you tell me something?'

'What is it?'

'Howcome you are a Mrs but you don't wear a wedding band?'

'Not that it's any of your business, but I am a widow. Good day to you, Mr Quentin.'

'And a great pleasure to make your acquaintance, widow woman.'

The weak sun was climbing higher as he leaned forward to follow her progress along the street. Immaculate carriage, long fine legs, radiating self assurance. Apparently Cardinal still had the flair for attracting class women, he reflected. Too bad for the marshal he couldn't hang onto them once he'd landed them.

But surely – neither could he?

That sickening thought ambushed him and the dark mood held him as he remained seated with the cigar fuming away forgotten between his fingers. When boot-heels clomped up the steps he raised his eyes to focus on the careworn features of Slow Joe Pierce.

'What do you want, lawdog? Or can I guess? Still running errands for Cardinal? Sure, what else would you do, a beat up old loser like you? Well, better make it quick and polite, Deputy.'

'Figured we should talk some about you and Miss Winters and how you're kind of upsetting things here, mister.'

Quentin rose to stand tall with long legs spread and his hands upon his shell belt drawing back the panels of the tailored black coat. Standing before him like that, he seemed both as big and dangerous a man as Slow Joe Pierce had ever confronted.

'Is that a mortal fact, Deputy?' His tone had an edge.

'What's here for you, mister? Everybody knows by now about you and the marshal and Miss Winters back in Dodge. You won and he lost out . . . fair enough. So why show here and stir things up for the marshal all over again? He took it on the chin from you both in Dodge. He didn't fuss when you took Miss Winters off of him, and he could have made it tough on you there if he'd wanted. But he left the victor the spoils and came up here to start again. Wouldn't you agree that adds up to playing the game clean and straight?'

Quentin's right hand now slid beneath the immaculately pressed left panel of his elegant jacket. He carried a shoulder holstered Smith and Weston .38 there, and sharp-eyed Slow Joe was aware of that fact. The deputy paled, staring into the flinty eyes fixed upon him. He made a nervous movement as though to back away, and Quentin instantly spread both hands with a mocking laugh.

He was empty-handed.

'Same old deputy. Cardinal's heel-dog with nothing going for him but being that. Well, you've done your job, little man, so you can head off back to the jailhouse and tell the marshal so. Tell him you've got me shaking in my shoes. You can also say I've got no hard feelings towards him and that I don't plan on troubling him here any longer than, say, a decade or two, top. You got all that, small-time?'

Slow Joe Pierce backed away down the steps.

Back in Dodge City he remembered how cool Quentin could appear under pressure, and then might explode into violence over next to nothing.

Somehow he screwed up the nerve to say, 'Better heed what I say, mister—'

He got no farther.

Quentin's backhander caught him hard to the side of the head and spilled him into the wagon ruts. 'Don't you tell me what I can do, loser!'

At that instant a door opened along the street and the unmistakable figure of the marshal appeared on the porch. Cardinal had been there for some time, having been alerted by a junior deputy that he thought Slow Joe intended paying a visit on Quentin. 'Just what the hell do you think you're doing, Quentin?'

He was coming down the steps as he spoke. He crossed at a swift, long-legged stride as the deputy struggled to his feet fingering a bleeding mouth.

'I'm sorry, Marshal . . . I didn't mean to—'

'Go see the doc.' Cardinal didn't take his eyes from Quentin, who appeared mildly amused as he leaned a shoulder against a porch support and hooked thumbs into a shell belt just above twin gun handles. The lawman's stare was cold. 'That why you came here, gunslick? To beat up men twice your age and half your size? Or maybe it was another reason? Why don't you tell me? Come on, you always had plenty to say as I recall.'

It was their first genuine face-off since Quentin had come to town. Cardinal sensed it was overdue.

'Well?' he rapped as the other just stared at him

in silence. 'You seemed full of talk just a minute ago when—'

'Thought we had a deal, Marshal.'

'What are you talking about?'

'How it played out in Dodge, is what, pilgrim. I won your woman off of you and you accepted it. Now this.'

'This what?'

'Don't play dumb. Somehow you conned Rebecca into dumping me and joining you so you could get to play kissy-face again!'

'You're talking trash. I had nothing to do with her coming here. I still don't know why she quit Dodge. We've barely sighted one another since she came and bought up the saloon.'

'Don't give me that. You—'

Quentin broke off, staring along the street. Cardinal turned to see a buggy with the fancy dun mare in the shafts coming their way. He recognized the slender figure of the driver straight off. He cut a look back at Quentin's face but the man's expression was unreadable as the snappy rig swung in then halted.

'I hope I've disturbed something.'

Cardinal saw that she was as self-possessed as ever today. He'd rarely seen Rebecca in any way disadvantaged in all their time together, come to think of it.

'You know, you could almost call this close enough for a family reunion, don't you agree, folks?'

Quentin's manner was mocking as he came

94

down the step to stand at Cardinal's side. Onlookers couldn't help but note how impressive both men appeared, nor how dangerous-looking in that loaded moment. 'Hello, Rebecca,' Cardinal said formally.

'Gene,' she nodded. 'I've been meaning to stop by.' Her gaze shifted to Quentin. 'I still can't believe you'd do a crazy thing like coming here, Ashley.'

'Hell, I'd do anything, Becky. Ask anybody. Shoot a priest, marry a fat lady from the circus . . . ride a hundred miles to check on somebody who might be playing me for a fool . . . anything. Don't you listen to the gossips?'

Before the woman could reply, Slow Joe and two junior deputies appeared from an alleymouth close by. Pierce had feared trouble might erupt here and had mustered reinforcements, just in case.

They were not needed.

As though reassured by the appearance of the lawmen, Rebecca nodded to both Cardinal and Quentin and drove away. Gene turned to Quentin but the man had already vanished back inside.

He fingered back his hat, was surprised to discover he was sweating. Then he grinned, realizing he'd rarely been happier to see Slow Joe's homey mug. He could not be sure how that scene might have played out had not the deputies shown when they did.

The mayor's brother was bouncing off the sturdy

walls of the saloon's back storeroom like something made of India rubber. Overweight, just like
the mayor, yet leagues lower down on the social
scale, Willis Julian was already bleeding from the
mouth and rasping asthmatically from the beating,
but there was no sign either from the two sweating
bouncers or from Branco and his smirking friends
that it was going to end soon, if at all.

'For Gawd's sake, Branco!' the man pleaded as he
hit the cement floor yet again. 'Fifty lousy dollars?
You'd do a man like this for a lousy half-century?'

The answer was a kick to the short ribs.

Desperately, the bloodied Julian seized hold of a
lower leg and sunk big horse teeth into the calf. A
bouncer yowled in agony and went reeling against
the wall, clutching the injured limb while his associate went to work on the biter with his stick.

Julian was halfway to his feet when the first heavy
blow landed. He pitched forward and struck the
floor with his face. Dimly, between the attacker's
legs, the unlucky gambler and tardy payer saw the
door begin to open. He dived between the legs,
somehow made it to his feet and charged for the
door just as Quentin entered with a cigar clamped
between his teeth. A red-faced Branco hollered,
'Stop that welching son of a mongrel dog!'

Quentin obliged, swaying to one side and thrusting out a well shod foot. Julian tripped, smashed
his unlucky head into the door edge and went
down like a sabotaged elevator.

In response to Quentin's enquiring look,
Branco came forward with a big phony smile.

'Just a slow payer, Ash. You know what they're like. What can I do for you?'

Quentin produced a folded bank check from a pocket of his brocade vest.

'Just wanted your OK on this,' he said, glancing at the sweating bruisers and Branco's well-dressed associates curiously.

'Monroe?' Branco said, glancing at the note. 'He's railroad, so his checks are OK here – even when they're not . . . if you know what I mean?' Branco's broad wink reinforced the well-known fact that he was busily courting the railroad in the hope of securing that spur line which stood to rake him in a fortune from real estate. Now was no time to come down too hard on any of the big players involved. 'Er, anything else, Ash?'

'Nope. Everything's going as smooth as silk at the tables.'

'One of the boys told me you were in some kind of nose-to-nose with the law earlier that you didn't mention—'

He broke off as the door closed slowly on Quentin's back. The financier, one of Branco's partners in the railroad scheme, glanced at Branco with raised eyebrows.

'Handles himself pretty uppity, that dude, Emil. Cool too. You know, we've been talking about him and wondering if—'

He broke off as Branco held a finger to his lips, then started out but paused at an afterthought. Branco came back and kicked the unconscious man in the short ribs. 'Oh yeah, when he comes around warn him against running to big brother about this. Tell him one squeak and I'll set Sy after him with a horsewhip.' He winked at his head bouncer. 'You make him believe I mean it, Sy.'

Big Sy Clanton ceased massaging his wounded leg, straightened and saluted. 'He'll believe it, boss, take my word.'

'He's a good man that Sy,' Branco stated absently as the four proceeded along the passageway to his spacious office. 'Only wish we could force the Grand West to ante up with that spur contract as easy as squeezing that fifty out of Julian,' he added, staring absently at a wall map of the region while the others helped themselves to his liquor.

'Don't you think it might be high time we started getting heavy with the line, Emil?' asked the financier, Tom Black. 'I mean, we've got a power of money and effort sunk into those farmers and their lousy twenty thousand acres of dirt out there. Could be Grand West needs a jolt along?'

Heads nodded and Branco stroked his chins.

'Meaning?' he grunted.

'Let's not beat about the bush, Mr Branco, sir,' urged the attorney, a timid runt with a vicious streak. 'We have been waiting for the railroad to come to terms and for something to maybe distract Cardinal away from our activities . . . waiting for all sorts of things, in truth. In the meantime we've got serious money outlayed and no guarantee we might not lose it all. We all agree with Tom. We've got to make things move on instead of waiting for them to happen.'

Branco asked quietly, 'What do you have in mind?'

'Their head engineer's the one that keeps throwing a spanner in the works at Grand West, so my spy tells me,' declared the realtor. 'Could be if that man should have an accident it would be to our advantage.'

A silence descended and Emil Branco sensed a change in the ancient game. He studied the faces about him. They'd obviously been discussing the frustrating impasse with the Grand West in which they found themselves, and decided it was time for action. He was excited by the prospect, yet vaguely uneasy.

He knew why.

His nerve had never been as it once was since Marshal Cardinal took over, a rare breed of lawman you could not bluff, buy or charm. The badgeman was every bit as committed to law and order as Branco was to the pursuit of the green-back dollar, which was going some.

He needed the Grand West operation to succeed but didn't mean to hang for it. But maybe it was time to start in taking some bigger risks.

'I'd rub that engineer out like that!' he commented, snapping his fingers. 'And it'd be easy enough to do. But I don't know about putting out a contract on him. You can't rely on gunners not to get caught, and not to sing like canaries when they do. And with Cardinal and his lousy deputies. . . .'

He was nibbling at the bait, but not actually biting yet.

'How about your Quentin?' the money man broke in unexpectedly, sallow cheeks flushed with excitement.

'What about him?' Branco challenged.

'We've all been watching him, Emil,' declared the realtor. 'Like, real close. And I've done some solid checking on his background, too. Mighty interesting, let me tell you. The picture I get is of a geezer who can't be beat with a sixshooter, who's hard as the hobbs of hell and is too damned smart about who he shoots and how, to risk running in with the John Laws. And on top of all that, he loves money and doesn't seem too delicate about how he makes it. He lives high, needs big dough and, maybe best of all, hates Cardinal's guts . . . likely over that good-looking woman though I'm only speculating about that. Still, I've a powerful feeling if you handed him a job he'd do it right.'

'Forget it.'

The fat man sounded dismissive.

But was he?

He took another slug of that mellow whiskey and blinked slowly.

'I'm curious about that threesome, you know,' he said thoughtfully. 'As near as I can figure the lawdog was set up cosy with that handsome female when Quentin showed and she fell for him. Some say she picked Quentin because he was rolling in cash after a long winning streak at the tables while the marshal was working for a lousy hundred a month and getting shot at every second weekend. That how you jokers heard it?'

Heads nodded and he continued.

'We advertised for a take-charge kind of lawman and Cardinal shifted up here leaving the love-birds to it. But eventually she sells up, kisses Quentin goodbye and moves here. Maybe she figured she made a mistake choosing Quentin? Who knows? Then after a few weeks Ash arrives . . . and I guess everybody including us has been trying to figure out who's dealing, winning, losing or skimming off the top in that three-cornered game ever since—'

'OK, OK, man,' the attorney with the hungry mouth cut in. 'Much obliged for the clarification. But where does that leave us? Sounds to me you've just laid out a clear picture of Quentin likely coming here looking to get his woman back . . . and the man'd have to be suspicious about finding her and the marshal back in the same town together again.' He spread his hands. 'Can't see why a body would have much difficulty siccing your dealer onto Cardinal under these circum-stances, if he was to wave a big wad of cash money under his nose. And it'd be a fair fight . . . all square and above board, and Quentin's reputation says he'd have to win. It's perfect.'

Silence held the room for a time, deep looks were exchanged. Every man knew he was testing deeper waters, yet each one wore the same hungry expression he could see on the man next to him.

It was surely time for the big play and the big win. Take control in Storytown and ram the rail-road deal through while the law office was still being run by Slow Joe Pierce.

Why not?

But Emil Branco still demurred.

'I've got Quentin slotted in here to work against the marshal, keep him wrong-footed and maybe even force him to quit in the long run if all this juicy hot gossip about himself and Cardinal and that flash female doesn't die down. To me, under-mining Cardinal and getting rid of him is every bit as important to us as the spur line deal itself now. With every day that passes I get the stronger and stronger notion that it's him I've got to fear more than any red-nosed goddamn railroad investigator. I ask you, what's the good of us burying a few fat railroad executives if Cardinal is still playing God and sniffing at our heels? Riddle me that!'

'Damnit it all, man!' the money man snapped, 'we just solved the freaking problem! Get rid of Cardinal.'

'And Quentin's got to be the man to do it,' the skinny attorney attested forcefully, greed and frus-tration raging now. 'Let's goddamn do it!'

'And I still say – no way – and I'm still the boss around here,' Branco cut in sharply, like slamming a door.

But there could be no telling, studying his face above his big frilled white shirt, whether a seed had been sown in Emil Branco's mind or not.

CHAPTER 7

WILD SIDE OF TOWN

None of those railroaders or local riff-raff brawling in the wagon yard in back of the saloon could fight worth a lick but they were swinging, cursing and getting knocked down regularly just as if they could.

'Turkeys!' Harry Slater snorted with a grin. 'I could whup them all together.'

'No you couldn't,' Cardinal said easily. 'You're a good rancher and a lousy fighter. We both know that.'

The cattleman grinned good naturedly as they turned their backs upon the mild violence outside.

'True enough, man,' he conceded, then was sober. 'But seems everyone's fighting everybody else these days . . . this feuding and fussing over the railroad is fixed to get a lot worse before it gets better, don't you reckon?'

'Bound to.' Cardinal shrugged. 'I smell big trouble brewing, but until something happens. . . .'

It was the quiet time in Dooley's Bar on Frontier Square in contrast to the carry-on outside. The early morning addicts had been in for their first heart-starters and left, the midday crowd was yet to show.

'What brings you to town, Harry?'

'Business, of course.'

'Don't lie. We both know Muriel handles all your business affairs.'

'You really know how to hurt a man. OK, I'll level. I want to know what's going on here with you and Rebecca and Quentin?'

'Nothing. Why?'

'Don't give me that, Gene. It was all over between you in Dodge when she dumped you for Quentin – sorry to bring that up. Then after all that time she shows, and now him. That doesn't figure and we both know it. So, level with a man.'

'You worry too much, Harry,' he said in a way that discouraged further comment.

Slater gave in easily. Turned out he had other things troubling him, personal things. He looked gloomy all of a sudden. 'That woman of mine. Would you believe I hired a horse-breaker last week and Muriel's got her flirty eye on him already?'

Cardinal held up both hands, palms forward.

'No. Not more of the same. We've been through all that and we're not doing it again. *Sabe*?'

To his surprise, Slater grinned. 'OK, OK, whatever you say. Anyway, I didn't come to town about that, just felt I wanted to talk about your situation.'

'OK, and we've done that. Do you know what we're going to do now?'

'What?'

'Jim!' Cardinal called to the bartender. 'Two more.'

That gray day when the winds of real trouble began blowing stronger across Storytown, started just like any other with clerks, housewives, children and tycoons, the rich and the poor alike, being awakened by the same familiar sound of creaking axles and slow-plodding hoofs indicating that regular-as-clockwork Quincey Halstrom was on his way to the river aboard his rusted water cart.

For Gene Cardinal, it began with the disciplined routine of shaving, dressing, checking out his Colt and rolling the first cigarette of the day upon the little railed porch of his second floor suite at the Clairmont.

The day's schedule was already mapped out in his mind; ride out to Cray Creek to talk to the farmers; visit Tadpole Ranch and maybe assign a deputy there to watch out for rustlers; prepare a report at the lawhouse to be presented at today's trial of a man accused of attempted murder; brief Slow Joe on the chores to be done that day while he was absent.

And not think about Rebecca.

That one slipped in under his guard, and

suddenly his hand-rolled tasted bitter to the tongue.

He didn't want to dwell on the mystery of recent events but it seemed he couldn't control his thinking just at that moment.

He'd loved her truly, another man had taken her from him; he liked to think he'd taken it like a man. He knew that his coming to Storytown and starting off fresh again had been the right move and in time the pain and bitterness had eased until it didn't hurt anymore.

Naturally he'd heard Rebecca and Quentin had split, but didn't feel much of anything one way or another. Why should he? Rebecca and he were all through a long time ago.

Next thing, she'd arrived in town and by the week's end had set herself up in the old French Palace now renamed the Rosetta. He was not sure how he felt about that, but had had no hesitancy in rebuffing what he took to be her advances. Thanks, Becky, but no thanks. Once down that painful road was enough. What was over was over.

Then, the gunfighter.

That was still a puzzle he was yet to fathom. Quentin and Rebecca had broken up in Dodge; everyone knew about it and she had confirmed it openly to him. So what prompted Quentin to come here, hang up his hat and act like he meant to stay?

He still didn't know what brought the man here, could only be certain it had to have something sinister about it.

When Quentin had first shown up in Dodge

he'd checked the files on the man as a matter of course, and that was even before the newcomer showed an interest in Rebecca.

He'd encountered records like that before. The West had more than its share of the gunfighter cum gambler cum fringe dweller of the owlhoot on its books for a lawman to identify the breed.

Quentin fitted the classification neatly. Yet several things set the man apart. He'd never been convicted of a major crime; the men he'd killed had died in duels where the law had no recourse to action. The man was considered dangerous, clever and a notorious ladies' man, but you couldn't hang anybody for that.

He'd swept Rebecca off her feet and suddenly Gene Cardinal had found himself looking around for another place to ply his lawman's trade.

He'd accepted the inevitable well, so he believed, but the way Rebecca had responded had left him bewildered at the time. He was always aware that there was a strange remoteness in her makeup which combined with her unusual strength of personality made her the most complex yet fascinating person he'd ever known. During their time together he'd never seen her appear afraid, penitent or even hurt, and this almost glacial disregard for his feelings when the axe finally fell had maybe hurt him most of all.

She continued to display most of those characteristics here in Storytown, but with one major change.

He'd sensed a hint of fear in her when she

arrived and was certain this had been accentuated uopn Quentin's arrival.

Did she fear this man she'd once loved? Why had he followed her if it was all over? And why did he sense Quentin was watching him as though waiting for something to happen?

He shook his head.

Plainly there were no answers. So he left quickly, clattering down the outside stairs and heading for the jailhouse as the first rays of the sun came rushing across the limitless plains from the east, its arrival coinciding with that of the Jimcrack Flyer from the north, clattering down the Grand West's tracks for the depot.

He didn't spare another thought for the former lovers of Dodge City. He had work to do.

Along at the Rosetta Saloon, Rebecca was already up and about, outwardly serene and unruffled. She was rarely seen any other way. It appeared to others that she'd worn the same shield of invincibility throughout the time she and Cardinal were lovers on the fabled streets of Dodge City – and nothing seemed to have changed, even when their glittering Camelot came crashing down.

The serene mask she displayed as she paused upon her balcony overlooking Dixie Street concealed everything – fear, cunning, all emotion. She had the ability to do that, no matter what her circumstances.

Circumstances had never appeared more dangerous.

From her bedroom window, she had glimpsed Gene riding out earlier, and had not sighted Ash Quentin since late the night before when she had seen the man making his way past her place along the far side of the street.

She was as outwardly unmoved by the man's continuing presence as she had been by his arrival, for that was her way. Yet the fear was there, real and immediate. For what he'd said to her in Dodge at the time of the breakup, which she had initiated, supported by his dramatic arrival here, had convinced her she had never been in such peril in her life.

His grim warning, issued in Dodge City, that he could not allow her to reject him – somehow appeared doubly menacing now the man had come to Storytown.

He'd even told her why he felt that way.

She had succeeded too well in making him love her. This had apparently never happened to the gunman-gambler before in all his womanizing life, and he was convinced it could never happen again. Therefore she must continue loving him, he had told her. He could not tolerate going back to the way he'd always been before they'd met.

But nobody told Rebecca Winters what to do.

To her surprise she'd found she could be frightened and it had been a combination of fear and self-preservation that had brought her to the decision to come to Cardinal's town.

She was still very much afraid. Yet she now still believed – with her understanding of the male species – that when killing day came, she would not be in peril.

She always survived no matter who else might go down.

Quentin rose at his customary gambler's hour of ten in his big room at the Mogul, upstairs above the main bar. He awoke alone. There was eager competition amongst the hotel's percentage girls to see who'd be the first to share the dashing gambler's bed, and Quentin had already been obliged to fend off the advances of more than one rich and bored housewife over recent days.

He barely saw the women here. He was on a one-track mission to unearth truth, identify the guilty, then do whatever brutal, bloody thing that was necessary to retrieve the status quo he'd once enjoyed in Dodge, and he would do it.

He dwelt obsessively upon their dazzling time together before the day Rebecca had calmly told him – just after they'd made love – that she did not love him and never had.

He might have begged her to take him back – but didn't know how.

But he did know how to throw the fear of God into her, as he'd done the previous night after climbing undetected to her balcony at the Rosetta and facing her down.

'What . . . what do you want, Ash?' She'd been scared yet poised.

'You know what. You and Cardinal. Why did you come here?'

'I love him and I asked him to defend me against a crazy man – you!'

'I figured that was what was going on.'

'He'll kill you if you hurt me. He told me so.'

'Don't bet money on that.'

Now, he couldn't believe he'd gone so far. He must be half loco!

He stared into the bureau mirror and saw a brooding figure with rippling muscles and sunken cheeks. Yet when he emerged from his room a half hour later to go dancing downstairs to breakfast, where he would flirt unabashedly with every female in sight, he was the epitome of the swash-buckling gambling man – an enigma wrapped up in a lethal riddle.

This only left Emil Branco of the four players destined to fill major roles in the coming days' events still abed. The girl whose name he could never seem to remember, had left earlier and another had just brought in his breakfast tray; hash browns, eggs easy over and a good slab of steak smothered in fried tomatoes.

Branco always ate well, yet some instinct warned that today he might well require additional suste-nance. As usual there were many things awaiting his attention, although by far the major concern was his problems with the Cray Creek farmers and the railroad. Those sodbusters from upper Key River were growing rebellious. Branco had promised he could persuade the Grand West to meet his inflated demands made on their behalf for access across their land for the spur line out to Cottonfield. There was still no hint of the railroad capitulating on that matter and it was possible the farmers might decide to do something stupid, such as approach Grand West to make a new low offer rather than risk missing out altogether.

Branco viciously speared a chunk of steak with his fork and raised his eyes to the window as the water cart creaked by, laying the eternal dust of Storytown.

The cold day wore on.

Gene Cardinal rode across the open range from Tadpole in the middle of the windy afternoon, making for Cray Creek.

The visit to Tadpole had taken longer than expected, involving a raid upon a suspected rustler hideout which had proven ineffectual, although there were indications that the law's increasing involvement out there could drive the cow thieves to seek safer pastures.

The farmers' communal house eventually raised itself above the level of the rolling prairies and he headed in at the lope. The moment he sighted the horses lined up at the hitchrail along one side of the plain plank building, he knew this was no ordinary day at Cray Creek. So far as he knew, these ragged-assed sodbusters never entertained, had few friends and certainly weren't part of the social fabric in Storytown.

So, who was visiting out here today? he mused. And wondered if it might have anything to do with the business which brought him here, namely the sodbusters' dealings with Grand West.

As he clattered up to the building a group of ragged urchins watched from the shade of a lone cottonwood. Life was tough out here for farmers from the hills of Kentucky and Tennessee. Gene couldn't figure why they were holding out against the railroad's attempt to string steel across their acreage for their spur line. He knew the Grand West was prepared to pay a fair price. He had heard a whisper that some third party was involved. And when he recognised the flashy buckskin belonging to Sy Clanton from the Mogul, he felt a flicker of suspicion.

He swung down and tied up, mounting unplaned steps.

He paused.

Raised voices sounded from within. Some kind of wrangle was taking place. Listening, he identified the voices of Wes Donald, farmer leader, and that of Branco's bodyguard and enforcer, Clanton.

There was an ante room off to one side of the lobby. He stepped inside and put his ear next to a crack.

'You guys are hicks, know that?' It was Clanton's deep voice. 'You leave the East on account you're losers, you damn near starve out here on your dirt because you can't figure prairie farmin'. Then you get a once-in-a-lifetime chance to strike it rich, and what do you do? Go to water so soon as the goin' gets tough, that's what.'

'We hear every day that Slater Belltrees is fixin'

to shelve the spur on account Branco demandin' too damned much,' protested a Kentucky twang.

Branco?

The marshal had heard enough. He went through to confront some dozen farmers in coveralls and straw hats, Sy Clanton and several Branco employees, along with his bespectacled attorney.

The voices dried up. Big Clanton bristled, greased mane glinting, his big hands clenched suddenly into fists.

'You double-dealin' bastards!' he accused the ragged farmers. 'You brought in the tinstars!'

'Tinstar, Clanton,' Gene corrected, moving deeper into the room, eyeing off the sodbusters. 'I'm alone. And nobody sent for me. Looks to me that the whispers my deputies have been hearing about town might hold water.'

'This is none of your put-in, Cardinal,' warned the husky Clanton.

'That's Marshal Cardinal to you, mister. And it sure is my business.' Cardinal fixed his gaze on the attorney, then cut to farmers' leader, Donald. 'Let me guess. You suckers are holding out for big railroad payments and Branco's right in the middle of the deal looking to make his usual usurer's cut.' He raised a hand as several made to speak. 'No, I'm not finished yet. From what I overheard, you fear you might miss out, and though I'm guessing here, Clanton, I'd like to wager your job is to rally the troops and keep them united. Right?'

As Sy Clanton glared at the marshal in silence, one of his men drifted to the windows to look out.

He turned and nodded to the big bruiser, who flexed big hands and smacked a fist into his palm.

'You know, Cardinal,' Clanton said deliberately, 'I've always had the notion that you walk far taller than you got any right to . . . like you're special or playin' God—'

He broke off and made a menacing move forward. Gene whipped out his Colt.

He had the drop and every man realized it.

But the marshal wasn't finished. When Clanton started towards him again, he struck with gunbutt and dropped the heavyweight to the floor.

Cardinal stepped back, holstered the piece and confronted the room.

'Anyone else share his views? Moran? Chaves? Milton? Come on, gentlemen, what will you tell Branco if you go back without at least some skinned knuckles to show you're earning your keep?'

They were gone within minutes, knuckles unskinned and Clanton lying groggily on his horse's neck, his face the color of old wallpaper.

The Cray Creek farmers stood in the dust looking bewildered, huddling together as though fearing it could be their turn next.

But Cardinal was now only interested in gathering information concerning Cray Creek and Grand West, which he had done by the time he eventually forked leather.

He wasn't sure whether what Branco was doing was illegal or not, but he knew it was extortionate and detrimental to progress.

'If Branco shows again, let me know,' he told Wes Donald.

'Sure, and, er . . . thanks, Marshal Cardinal,' muttered the farmer leader. 'Er . . . I think?'

The journey back was uneventful and the city lights were showing through the dusk as the weary-legged horse carried him towards the Key River bridge.

Riverboats and freight barges cluttered the levees and tar barrel torches were being lighted all along the dockside. The lights revealed a little dust still hanging in the air despite Quincey Halstrom's best efforts. The water carter could nail most of the dust but never quite got the lot. That could be a lot like law work. No matter how many you bagged, buffaloed, jugged or bottled, there were always a few left to make life hazardous for a man with a star.

He hit Dixie and traveled along it through the slums, which gradually gave way to more solid buildings and commercial premises. Suddenly he reined in at a sound, cocked his head to identify shouting voices and a crashing noise, like furniture being hurled about.

He raked with spur upon realizing something was happening out back of the Rosetta.

Quentin had come to the old abandoned harness shed across from the Rosetta during the afternoon, after quitting the gaming tables and the fuggy atmosphere of the finest saloon in town.

He often came here, although mostly by night.

He would sit on a rough old bench which threatened to snag his twenty-dollar pants and just watch the saloon, waiting for glimpses of Rebecca, just like some love-struck loser, so he thought.

He must have proof she'd dumped him for Cardinal. He wanted that full certainty along with all the pain that accompanied it, before he could do what he must. . . .

Customers going in.

He peered through a cobwebbed window as a party of railroad workers mounted the steps of the saloon and marched right in.

Even rail laborers, losers and grifters, were free to march in there any time they wanted, providing they behaved themselves and didn't eat up all the peanuts and cheese.

All but him.

He slowly massaged his face as memory again conjured up images of their time together. . . .

Just one brief part of a single year out of his thirty, that had proved worth living! The only time in his life he'd ever truly loved – finished with just a few cold words from her. Leaving only the rage and the need to lash back, like an animal, a force inside too huge to fight. . . .

He was jolted alert by the loud voices of the trio arriving to slake their dry across the street and quickly vanishing into the warm, lamp-lit interior.

Again he lost track of time until some brawler was knocked clear through a front window of the saloon opposite in a shimmering, tinkling cascade of shivering glass fragments.

A brawl. Who the hell cared?

Then he heard a woman scream – maybe Rebecca – and he was out of the door and running.

It was the buffalo hunters.

He realized this the moment he shouldered through the batwings where men thrashed and roared about on the floor amongst broken furnishings while another bunch of wild and hairy ones punched and gouged their way along the bar front, fighting like men who'd never enjoyed anything so much in their lives before.

Nobody seemed to notice him as he came in lightly, ready for anything. Rebecca stood behind her bar staring with arms folded and chin held high, looking like royalty reviewing her vassals at their worst.

He shook his head. You had to hand it to her. She was unlike any woman he'd ever known and had so many qualities that were exceptional. Unfortunately, one was a belief that she could cut any man just when she damn-well felt like it. Wrong! Nobody but nobody cut Ash Quentin.

He suddenly realized she had seen him. Her expression was unmistakable. Despite everything, she was plainly expecting him to settle the trouble.

In an instant he was the old swaggering Ash Quentin again, not some wounded night animal licking its wounds in the dark.

The first Beard never knew what hit him.

Flinging drinkers aside Quentin nimbly reached the hunters to lay one out with the best punch seen in the entire fight thus far.

The second Beard roared like a wounded buffalo and hurled himself upon Ash's back, free hand trying to gouge his eyes. Quentin's elbow slammed backwards and caught the Beard in the groin, dropping him to the floor like a typhoid case amongst spilled liquor and cigar butts.

Another came after the gambler, arms flailing like a windmill.

Next instant the hunter found himself leaning upon the muzzle of the Smith and Wesson Quentin had palmed from its shoulder holster and shoved into his guts.

'Jest what a man would expect of a white-fingered dude pimp!' the Beard mouthed. 'The sneak. Show me one stinkin' dude that don't tote one of them th—'

'Out!'

Ash lifted the gun and slammed the butt fully into the man's mouth, stepping back to avoid the spray of crimson and flying teeth. 'Now!'

'No, Ash, no guns!'

Intimidated by the weapon, the brawlers turned to water in a moment. Ash appeared nonchalant as he prodded them outside then swatted the ring-leader flat with gunbutt and kicked him off the gallery into the muddied wagon ruts.

Unexpectedly, a man landed on his back and whipped an arm about his throat. In an instant Quentin had flipped him over his head to land atop the other, both slipping and sliding in the slush.

So far so good.

Trouble was, Quentin kept belting the last man even though it was plain to everyone this hellraiser was all through. Whether the gambler didn't want to stop or couldn't, was unclear. He kept battering the howling figure until the man's face was a bloody pulp.

Now there were others trying to pull him off but they couldn't stop him until suddenly a .45 shoved itself into the gambler's contorted face and a familiar voice shouted, 'Enough, Quentin. This is the law!'

It was the marshal. Quentin threw a lightning hook but the marshal was even quicker. The gunbarrel slammed against his temple and he slumped unconscious across the buffalo hunter's battered body.

CHAPTER 8

LOVERS OF DODGE CITY

'Oh, Gene, will he be all right?' she asked anxiously.

'He's OK.'

'He certainly doesn't look it.'

'I had to stop him before he used that gun.'

Cardinal stepped back to stare down upon the unconscious Quentin who'd been placed on a side porch bench illuminated by a dim door lamp. The buffalo hunter's friends had toted him off uptown to the medico's but it was decided Ashton would not require further treatment after he came to.

Gene took out his tobacco and rested his weight on one leg, a cigarette paper pasted to his lower lip.

121

Rebecca folded her arms, a characteristic gesture he well remembered.

'Did you know about Ash's violent reputation in other places when I was falling for him in Dodge?'

'Yes.'

'Yet you never said anything to me?'

'No.'

'Why not?'

He glanced away. The reason he'd remained silent back in Dodge had been pride. He'd not been prepared to use such information against Quentin in order to try to win her back. Personally, it had seemed the right thing to do, but professionally he'd likely been at fault.

'Has he ever killed anybody? He told me he had.'

He ignored that query. He had another he suddenly needed an answer to.

'Why did you come here, Rebecca? I mean, really?'

'Very well, if you must know, I came here for your protection. There, I've admitted it and I'm not apologizing.'

'Protection?'

'From Ash.' Her calm expression faltered a little as she looked down on the man, who was beginning to stir. 'He . . . threatened to kill me if I didn't go back with him. I know he meant it. . . .' She put a hand on his arm and stared up into his face. 'Gene, I also told him I'm still in love with you. I was desperate, afraid. Do you understand?'

'How did he react?'

'By following me down here. I never anticipated that. I thought, after my telling him that
lie, he would be too proud to do anything but
walk away. But I do believe he's crazy in a way
and—'

Quentin groaned and sat up abruptly. Despite
his grogginess the gambler was already lurching to
his feet on the boards even before he could see
straight.

'Where is that redheaded sonuva—' he began,
then broke off. He stared. 'By Judas, it wasn't old
hairy-face! It was you who decked me, Cardinal.'
He raised fingers to his head, felt the bandage
Rebecca had placed there and lurched erect.
'You'll pay for that, lawman.'

Rebecca got between them, still outwardly calm.

'Stop this, Ashton. Hasn't there been enough
trouble here for one night.'

But he moved her gently aside, eyes drilling into
the marshal.

'Couldn't resist the temptation, could you,
Cardinal? A gold-plated chance to show yourself
the big hero again in front of her ... at my
expense. Well, try it fair and square now, lover
boy!'

'You've got that wrong, mister—' Cardinal
began, then bobbed as a whistling fist grazed off
his forehead.

His response was automatic. Quentin was still sick
and seeing double while the marshal was primed
and ready. One short powerful punch to the jaw was
all it took and the gambler would have hit the

boards again had Gene not caught his sagging body.

'Take him to the jailhouse,' he ordered some bystanders. They responded instantly and Gene bent to retrieve his hat.

Rebecca placed a hand on his arm, her eyes as large, dark and warm as he remembered.

'It was terrible of me to come here, I know it, Gene. But I had no other choice. I feared for my life and you were the only hope I had. You . . . you still care for me, don't you, Gene?'

He didn't respond because he couldn't. Everything was happening too fast. He simply looked into her eyes a moment, then nodded and left to follow the four men toting Ash Quentin to the lockup.

They occupied a rear alcove off the Mogul's gaming rooms, the farmers, three floor men, a battered Clanton and Branco himself. Branco was savaging a whole roast chicken and scowling at everybody in sight. The customers were wisely giving the alcove a wide berth even though they'd have liked to have heard what was going on between Mr Big and the Cray Creek sodbusters. And was it true that the marshal had clashed with Quentin earlier? And how about the rafter rattler at the Rosetta if one was looking for another heady topic?

It wasn't really like conversation, more like a diatribe with Branco spitting out venom and chicken bones with equal spleen as he reiterated the facts of life to Wes Donald and the two farmers who'd accompanied him to the city to confer with the big man whom they thought of now as a 'former' business associate.

Cardinal had sobered every single Cray Creek resident earlier that day.

His intervention at the meeting, his comments on the hitherto secret deal, but most of all his quelling of the Rosetta brawl and the handling of the lethal Quentin, had frightened the men of the land and had them now looking for a way out.

They wanted Branco to let them off the hook in order that they might quietly close a low-profit deal with Grand West and simply let it go at that.

But Branco was threatening paybacks and nightriders and crop-levellings and ugly things that could happen to farmers' families when they were away from home. He was preaching the gospel of fear and made the overall situation perfectly clear. The jittery farmers would stick to their original agenda or Uncle Emil would surely have their balls.

But he was making a big mistake.

He was talking like a man still holding top cards without acknowledging that much had changed. The marshal knew of their plan to gouge Belltrees, and had warned them what could happen if they persisted. There could be little doubt he would come calling at the Mogul before he was much older.

The others saw it as time for a graceful retreat.

But Branco either could not or would not see it.

So he kept ranting until Wes Donald finally rose and said, 'Sorry you feel this way, Mr Branco. But we're through and jest stopped to tell you so. Let's go, boys.'

A choleric Branco shouted at them to halt but the farmers had had enough. Branco whipped out a derringer and triggered into the ceiling. The farmers took to their heels and ran all the way to the jailhouse.

Gene pressed finger and thumb against the corners of his eyes as he paced to and fro before the Mogul's long bar, boot-heels rapping loudly where normally such sounds would be swallowed up by the noise of the crowd.

There was no longer any crowd left at the Mogul, just Branco and several staff along with Marshal Cardinal, Slow Joe Pierce and three griping farmers.

Branco had explained at length that he'd not shot at anybody but simply for effect, which might or might not be true.

Cardinal had ordered the place cleared the moment he arrived.

It was highly possible Branco might have been let off with just a warning, but for one factor. His mouth. Fat Emil stood to make serious money from the Grand West scam and couldn't believe the difficulties, he had encountered. He'd hoped to come to terms with Slater Belltrees tonight, yet here he was with recalcitrant sodbusterss; a beat-up enforcer; a hysterical dancer complaining about one itty-bitty gunshot and his head dealer with a bandage around his skull.

While it seemed to Branco he was being expected to crawl to the law.

He wouldn't do it.

'If you want to know the truth, I'm up to here with your persecution, Cardinal,' the fat man suddenly erupted. He threw both arms wide. 'A whole damn city and a million miles of prairie for you to go glory-hunting in, but you've got to persecute me. Well Emil Branco isn't going to take it anymore. First thing in the morning I'm going to file a harassment suit against you and I'm going to make it stick.'

Gene was now leaning against the bar.

It had been a long day for him on the plains, taking into account rustler hunting, enforcing the law out at Cray Creek and then the clash with Quentin topped off by that scene with Rebecca.

All that. Now this.

He'd known for some time most of the town's real troubles had their genesis here at the Mogul. He felt relieved now he could see what had to be done.

'You're shut down until further notice, Mr Branco,' he announced. 'You will be obliged to reapply for your license before Judge Harris, and you might as well know I'll be making it as tough as I can to prevent you getting it.'

Branco appeared to deflate before their eyes. But his voice was vicious and full of hate. 'You're all through, Cardinal,' he croaked like a sick old bullfrog. 'From here on in it's you and me, and you are going to find out just what a little man you really are for somebody who likes playing God.'

As Gene lighted up he thought about Quentin at the jailhouse with a vague unease. He brushed this aside as he turned away to supervise the closing of the city's finest saloon.

Gene said, 'You're free to go, mister.'

Quentin adjusted the bandage to his head which Slow Joe had applied. He was pale but formidable, standing there beneath the drop light. Gene leaned forward casually, picked up the man's gunbelt and passed it to him.

'What's the charge?' he growled, buckling the rig around his middle.

The marshal leaned back in his swivel chair, raised his boots to the desk. 'No charge.'

'Don't do me any favors, Cardinal.'

'No favors, just a warning.'

'Let me guess – stay away from Rebecca?'

'On target.'

'What'd she tell you?'

Cardinal stared straight up into the man's eyes. 'That you couldn't take her dumping you and that you followed her here meaning to do her harm.'

'You think I'll deny it?'

'Are you saying it's true?'

'What I'm saying ... is you go fry in hell, Cardinal. And keep something in mind. Next time we cross swords, you won't get the jump like you did tonight.'

The door was shouldered open and he was gone, footsteps echoing away to silence.

It was quiet for a long moment before the deputy spoke.

'What now, Marshal?'

'Why, coffee of course. What do you think?'

CHAPTER 9

THE LONG NIGHT

She was always first abroad at the saloon and today
was no exception. Her regular routine was to rise,
attend to her toilet, braid her long dark hair
before the oval looking glass in her office cum
quarters upstairs and then make her way downstairs.

It was her favorite time of day, this hushed early
morning when the world seemed clean and fresh
in that magical hour before greed, lust, hatred and
violence got to tarnish it again.

Yet as she paused she realized that however she
might strive to make this day feel the same as any
other since coming to the city, it was very different.

Last night's events had made the change.
Coming face to face with Quentin again, Gene's
arrival, the brawl.

Her hand gripped the banister tightly. She'd
hoped her coming to Storytown in itself might

130

have settled her troubles and banished her fears. Instead her situation appeared even more dangerous. Quentin was looming as a greater threat by the hour. She wished she could depend on Gene to protect her but somehow he had not responded in the personal totally-protective manner she'd anticipated. Playing the big cards, she'd at least hinted she still loved the marshal, expecting him to be elated, but instead his response had been reserved.

She wondered if he suspected. . . ?

Perhaps she had played her willful games once too often. That knowledge haunted her every day now. All her life she'd used people, embraced and discarded them on a whim, had gone onto the next man or the next adventure without a backward glance.

She had always used her beauty as a weapon, had had men falling at her feet all her life. Her infatuations never lasted; they were, after all, only infatuations.

When she had first laid eyes upon Ash Quentin it had been the finish of Gene. She had thrown him over without a second thought and those months with the gambling man had been ecstatic.

They were also limited.

The day came when she had to tell him it was over – and a black day it turned out to be. For unlike his predecessors, the dangerous Quentin refused to accept it. As far as she could fathom, it was the first time in his thirty years the gambler had ever known love or anything like it. He was hurt, incredulous, enraged.

Then came the threats, her own fears, and she knew she must take action. Quentin was insane enough to kill her – she couldn't stop him.

But she knew someone who could.

It had taken courage to come to Storytown, and Gene had not reacted as she'd hoped. But she had still managed to implement her plan to play on Quentin's suspicions and jealousy with the intent of shifting the man's focus from her to Gene Cardinal – after which she could simply step back and let events take their natural course.

The two must eventually fight, she still believed. And having loved and lived with both intimately, she truly believed Gene had the greater strength and character and sheer ability with the guns to come out the winner.

That could be the only outcome she would hear of.

She would be safe and free again, could put it all behind her, then put on her prettiest dress and confidently wait for the next handsome man to see her and fall in love.

This vision slowly faded and she was back to the reality of the here and now.

Quentin was the unpredictable factor.

She could never be sure if the man was crazy with jealousy, or simply crazy. She was troubled by nightmare visions of his going completely off the rails and killing her and going after Gene.

Whether Quentin's obsessive actions were sane or otherwise didn't really matter at this late hour, she supposed. If she thought she could have him killed she would do it without a second thought. He was frightening her and she would never forgive him for that. Yet he was still in town and she was still here, trapped in her own place and unsure that when she went downstairs he might not be there with a gun and a fake regretful, 'You should never have dumped me, baby. We were meant to be forever.'

Bang!

She shuddered. Not a gunshot – just a door slamming in the wind.

But the fright had sobered her and cleared her thinking. She was allowing herself to teeter on the edge of panic. Think only of the reality! Her plan was surely still operative. No good reason to fear Quentin might jump the gun and simply murder her. He was so vain and proud that he must deal with Gene first, surely. Reviewing her situation almost calmly once again, her daring plan was plainly working like a charm.

Why, they'd even come to blows already.

Who could tell when blows might become gunshots . . . and she would wager her saloon that Gene Cardinal must walk away from that antici-pated clash leaving her tormentor where he should be right now . . . in his grave.

She spat a vicious curse then straightaway stopped to breathe deeply and put on her Queen Nefertiti mask.

Rebecca . . . always in control . . . no matter who else might lose theirs, their way or their very lives.

The staff had worked until 3 a.m. cleaning up after the ruckus. Two windows were boarded over along with one mirror, but apart from this the Rosetta didn't appear too much the worse for wear.

She went through to the galley to fix herself the first cup of life-giving coffee of the day: froze.

Glowing from a cut-glass vase upon the cold range and catching the window light was a huge bunch of flowers with daisies predominating. Her favorites.

Her eyes flew about the room to focus on the partially opened back door. A wisp of tobacco smoke drifted through. With one hand to her breast, aware of the thudding of her heart, she went through the galley and opened the door fully as Quentin rose from the porch bench.

He was immaculate as usual; she'd rarely seen him any other way. He'd removed the strapping around his head, although a vicious bruise still showed at the temple.

He was smiling, graceful, frightening.

'Ash, what . . . how. . . ?

'Just wanted to surprise you, honey. You know old light-fingers. I can get in anyplace . . . produce just as many aces as you want. Pleased to see me?'

'No . . . no I'm not, to be truthful. And why the flowers?'

'I always brought you flowers, honey.'

'When we were together.' She looked him straight in the eye. She was agitated but it didn't show. Self-discipline. That was something she had learned from Cardinal. He was so responsible and

134

self-disciplined at times that it had driven her into the arms of another man.

And she thought: who am I trying to fool with that one?

'Ashley, why did you follow me here? Admit the real reason.'

'Heck, lady, I thought you'd be flattered and—'

'Why should I be? We broke up because it was impossible for us to continue another minute. That was months ago. What on earth could make you believe that by coming here to Storytown and all this uproar, that anything would change? I simply can't understand that.'

She was impressed by her own demeanour and delivery. She sounded like a college-educated college principal dealing with ill-mannered undergrads.

He advanced on her wordlessly and she felt the treacherous bite of fear again.

In a way, she was amazed to be still alive. In Dodge, he'd threatened he would kill her before he'd let her go. He'd meant it; she'd seen it in his eyes. Yet when she'd planned her flight to Storytown he had calmed for some reason, possibly sadistic. Maybe he'd planned to permit her to run in terror to Cardinal – as she did – then deal with her.

But getting here had given her a chance at least to renew her connection with the marshal and busy her desperate self in diverting a killer's attention to another.

His eyes told her nothing now but she prayed

those bruises and the humiliation he'd suffered last night at the marshal's hands might succeed in transferring his sick obsession totally from herself to Gene.

His eyes searched her face.

'So beautiful and so controlled. . . .' he whispered. Then his smile flashed. But it was entirely bogus, and Rebecca knew it. This was the smile he used to cover a hurt or to disguise his real intentions. He had never hurt her but the fear was always there. It had never been more excoriating – yet she had never appeared more calm.

'Either kill me or leave my place – you – you loser!'

She couldn't believe she had said that. For a moment his face was alight with a titanic rage, yet the look was quickly gone.

'You do still love him,' he breathed. He nodded. 'I knew it all along. Well, this puts a different slant on things. It means he stole you back as I suspected the moment you told me you were through. He went under my neck and—' He had trouble speaking, so intense was his emotion. 'You both made me look a fool and nobody does that and lives to brag about it . . . nobody!'

'I want you to leave.'

He stared at her. She stood very tall and erect before him, achingly lovely but remote and austere before turning to walk away.

He appeared to stumble as he went down the steps then bumped a door jamb, so enraged he could not see clearly.

And in the gloom of the galley, the woman stood with her back against the closed door, head tilted upwards, whispering fiercely,

'Kill him, Gene. Only you can . . . you owe that to me. . . .'

Cardinal looked up from his bookwork.

'What's that racket out front?' he said.

'That, Marshal,' replied Slow Joe, working on his third mug of joe, 'is the sound of trouble.'

'When I ask a straight question I want a straight answer. You're not playing to the gallery in the show-up room now, mister. What?'

The deputy stood reproved.

'Er, sorry, Gene. What you hear are some riff-raff on the other side of the street toting placards objecting to the closing down of the Mogul. You want us to go disperse them?'

Cardinal completed his entry in the ledger, dusted drying powder over the ink, closed the book and rose to his feet. He went out onto the long front porch where two deputies sat staring across the street. Pierce ranged up behind him and said, 'Mostly hired trouble from up the river. For a dollar an hour you can get some folks to do almost anything at a time like this, I guess.'

He moved farther out into the feeble sunshine in order that the mob of protesters might see him clearly. Their chanting slowly faded. Several shook their fists at him yet without conviction. He was given the impression they were ready to take to flight should he but step down into the street.

Apart from the rented mob the street appeared unusually quiet. Not empty, just quiet. He'd checked on the square earlier and that had been the same. Emil Branco was taking his protest against the closure of the Mogul very seriously, it appeared. His employees were in evidence all over town, promoting the fat man's point of view, soliciting support and doing a professional job of bad-mouthing the city marshal.

He'd kicked over an ants' nest last night. Branco was the most powerful man in the city and today a very angry one. He had plenty of people in his pocket and seemingly unlimited funds available to buy support which he might otherwise have been unable to attract. The wheeler-dealer plainly meant to carry this fight all the way to the law office, and Storytown was intensely uneasy about it.

The closure of the Mogul had eclipsed last night's violence at the Rosetta, although that also was occupying the man in the street today. A time of unrest had descended upon the plains city and its marshal was ready to meet it head-on.

'Clear them off!' he ordered suddenly. 'They require a permit for public assembly and they haven't got one.' He turned to Pierce. 'Send out the patrols, Slow Joe. Any groups of six or more are to be dispersed. Well, what are you waiting for, man?'

'Er, nothing, Marshal, nothing at all. All right you lawmen, you heard the marshal. Let's hustle.'

Cardinal had trained his men well. He stood watching with satisfaction as the deputies formed a human chain and began sweeping the placard-bearers away. One objected and got an elbow under the brisket for his trouble. The street was looking peaceful again by the time Gene turned to go inside, when his eye picked out the saloon swamper in the striped pink shirt heading his way from across the square.

The man was from the Rosetta and he brought a note for Marshal Cardinal from Miss Winters.

She wished to see him.

He stood in the sun frowning for a minute before going inside to get his hat. It was still cold by the time he reached the square and the sun upon his shoulders held no warmth. As he turned the corner out of the street he glimpsed an altercation between two deputies and several Mogul staffers across the way. He paused until the deputies gained the upper hand and had herded the troublemakers away with their clubs. He nodded in approval and kept on. He'd anticipated trouble, although not quite on this scale. Yet he welcomed the situation. Branco had been over-reaching himself of late; too successful and too greedy. It was time the city found out who was really running things, and it was not Branco nor his money.

It was the man with the badge who was still in charge as he continued to the designated meeting spot.

This was the same Gene Cardinal who had dominated Dodge City, Pioche, Haggerstown and Channahan, South Dakota, over the past decade.

Today he appeared almost the same as he had done on any working day in any of a dozen trouble towns. Almost, but not quite. If there had ever been a chink in his armor it was the woman he was on his way to meet in back of Harper's General Store.

There was a fountain and an open table and bench area in back of the store where clerks and others liked to take their lunch under the shade trees.

Rebecca was seated on a bench in a plain white dress which on her naturally looked sensational. He paused to stare across at her, feeling a slow-fading tightness in his chest. She was the one card in the Storytown deck he'd never expected to be called upon to play. He was still no clearer as to whether he was happy or dismayed to have her here, than he'd been on the day of her arrival. There was a sense of detachment deep inside him which he had never experienced before and as yet had failed to understand.

'It was good of you to come, Gene. I didn't know if you would or not.'

'What is it, Rebecca?' He didn't sit. His arms were folded and he appeared remote.

She looked up at him and said, 'I have come to warn you.'

'About?'

She glanced around. She was afraid and it showed. He had never seen her actually fearful before. And nor, for some weird intuitive reason, had he ever felt more remote from this beautiful, but essentially unknowable woman.

'Ash,' she said at length, rising. She looked into his eyes. 'I believe Ash is going to try and kill you.'

'What makes you say that?'

'We just had a terrible scene. Naturally your name came up. He . . . he believes I left Dodge and came here because I still love you.'

'And do you, Rebecca?'

She reached up and touched his face.

'Of course I do, darling. I thought you knew that. Why else would I have sold up and come all this way?'

'Fear?'

'What?' she frowned, stepping back. 'Fear of what?'

'Not what, who, Rebecca. You're afraid of Quentin. I sensed it from the day he first appeared. You see, when you love someone and live with them, you get to know all about them – or at least a lawman does. You were afraid when you first came, you were more so when Quentin showed, you are close to terror right now.'

She appeared speechless. She'd always prided herself on her subtlety, her ability to deceive, to act, to pretend. She had overlooked the fact that a man like this, in his profession, encountered deception every day of his working life.

'So, was it fear that brought you here, Rebecca?' he went on. 'You dumped the wrong man – a man with a record for never forgiving anyone who does him wrong? And when you were afraid enough, did you come up with the clever idea to come to me and maybe give Quentin the impression that we were together again? Did you hope that that killer might shift his anger and hurt from you to me – and then sit back and watch me deal with him and so save your life? How close am I to the truth . . . honey?'

She was ghostly pale, stunned by his attitude and perception.

Her dominant reaction now was fear. Fear that what he'd accused her of might mean he would not fill the role she had planned for him even before quitting Dodge City. Her loving protector. But there was no sign of love in his face or manner now. He seemed angry. What if he deserted her?

'Gene, what else could I do? He's crazy. I couldn't just wait for something awful to happen to me, could I?'

'No. But you could have come to me and asked me to help, not deceived me and tried to trick me into—'

'But I've just told you everything now—'

'You had to . . . only when you had to. You had to make sure I was alerted so Quentin couldn't jump me, so that I'd be ready to fight when the time came.'

'Please, Gene, please, won't you—'

'Save the tears, Rebecca. And . . . and nobody's going to kill you.'

'Oh, Gene, you're wonderful!' she cried, clutching at his arms and shaking with relief. He'd never seen her more beautiful yet that meant nothing to him. His feelings didn't change when she stood on

142

tiptoes and kissed him full on the mouth. Once, that would have been about the most exciting thing he could have imagined. Right now, he was only wondering whether she thought Quentin was watching them and whether seeing them kiss would add to the gunman's rage at losing her, add that extra edge to his hatred . . . and maybe his gunspeed.

Sweat glistened across the smooth landscape of Emil Branco's moon face as he thrust his head from his office door and hollered, 'Where the hell is Clanton? Sy? You there Sy?'

His voice echoed through an almost empty barroom. Three Mogul staffers sat perched on stools at the long bar with a fourth pulling beer for them, this, in a saloon which could normally boast a hundred customers at that time of day.

'He went off someplace an hour ago, boss,' a scrawny case-keeper answered. 'Kinda broody, I thought he was. Got somethin' eatin' at him, has Sy, I reckon. Got a hunch it might be the way he gets cut down to size by Cardinal each time he sticks his head up lately. That kind of thing can eat at a tough *hombre* like Sy.'

'What makes you think I'm interested in his troubles, mister?' Branco mouthed, making his bad-tempered way through empty tables and chairs. He threw a gesture at the tightly-barred front doors. 'That stiff-necked marshal is kicking my people off the streets, and they're sending an auditor around some time today to go over my books. You all know what's going on, don't you? Last night's hooraw was just an excuse for Cardinal to open up with all his artillery. He shut me down, the sonuva, and now he thinks he's moving in for the kill. So don't give me any gaff about poor old Sy. Gimme a brandy!'

The murmur of Dixie Street traffic filtered through shuttered windows into the quiet room. Nobody wanted to speak for fear of irritating their employer further. Branco might even be scared, for there were secrets in his closet and he would never survive their exposure to the harsh glare of inspection.

The fat man twitched at the sound of smashing glass, jerking his eyes to the ceiling.

'What the hell was that?'

'Guess it's him,' the bartender said. 'Quentin.'

Branco stared at the man.

'What would that one be doing up there?'

'Beats me,' the man replied. 'Came in lookin' like sudden death and went up to his room. Every now and then he busts somethin'. Somethin' ridin' him hard, boss. Don't ask me what.'

Branco raised both hands heavenward then dropped them to meaty thighs with a slap of disgust.

'Wonderful! First Clanton, now the dealer. I pay that dude a king's ransom and I treat him with kid gloves on account he hates Cardinal's guts and I need a hotshot like that on my side right now. And what happens? Cardinal shuts me down and Quentin dives for cover. I must have killed a black

144

cat and don't know it. I need that gun-tipper on deck today, here, right by my side.'

'I wouldn't push that if I were you, Emil,' advised a second man. 'I seen him come in. He looked like a man who would eat nails and spit 'em onto your coffin lid.'

'The hell you say,' Branco said with a sudden burst of energy, hurling himself off his stool and making for the stairs. 'Today I need every man and I'm calling in all my markers. Quentin owes me and he's about to find that out.' He paused at the newel post to wag a fat forefinger. 'And when Clanton shows, tell him from me if he wanders off again between now and when I finish with Cardinal, I'll skin him and fire him in that order.' He shook his head in disgust as he started to climb. 'Tough guys? They've got to be kidding.'

CHAPTER 10

MAN AGAINST MAN

Looking for a man, Marshal Cardinal walked Dixie Street neither fast nor slow, but as usual. On the surface the town appeared calm enough but he wasn't fooled. Danger was in the air. He could smell it and feel it. And yet he was calm. For that was his job, always to be calm and in control.

Wasn't it?

He appeared deep in thought as he turned the haberdasher's corner and he didn't see the powerful figure standing in the doorway of the poolroom. But he did hear the swift stutter of boots on plankwalk and wheeled sharply to see Sy Clanton rushing at him looking as big as a freight train and swinging a length of iron pipe.

Gene barely had time to duck to one side as the pipe came whistling down, missing his shoulder

146

but catching his leg a painful glancing blow.

Clanton whirled with surprising agility, despite a skinful of booze, and launched another charge, his face a mask of brute determination.

Cardinal might have drawn his Colt, but didn't. Setting himself squarely now, he let the bruiser come to him, slipped inside the swinging pipe and smashed into the ugly face behind a pile-driving shoulder.

The crash of Clanton's two-forty pounds landing on the broad of his back carried a long way. The marshal stood over the unconscious figure with weak sunlight glinting from his badge, wanting them all to see and remember what they saw. If this was developing into the long anticipated show-down between the law and Emil Branco, he wanted the people to witness this scene and absorb the lesson of the outcome between the law's toughest, and theirs.

He summoned a passing drover and had him tote the bloody-faced bodyguard round to the jail-house where a beaming Slow Joe Pierce was more than happy to provide Clanton with a cell, there to await tonight's line up in the show-up room.

But all exuberance faded from the law office later when Gene sat his men down and quietly gave them the news.

He told them he had good reason to believe Ash Quentin was looking for him with a gun, and that he intended to patrol the town alone until they met up.

They told him he was loco.

Slow Joe insisted on accompanying him on his patrol or, failing that, at least to get to set up watches to ensure he wasn't bushwhacked.

Both offers were rejected. Gene might have easily identified this situation as routine policing work requiring the full support of his lawmen. But it felt totally personal. Quentin would not be here with a gun if they'd not loved the same woman, he reasoned. His intention now was to have Quentin behind bars facing charges before this day was done. If it didn't work out that way, well, he didn't want to risk good men maybe getting killed while he settled what was, after all, his personal affair.

He walked out, pausing only to loose his .45 in its holster several times before moving west along Dixie.

Slow Joe's immediate reaction was to fumble in a desk drawer and gurgle down half a flask of rum. And he hated the stuff.

Smoke trickled lazily from Quentin's lips.

He was dressed in his finest and his thick hair was brushed until it shone like polished silver. His hotel room was neat and quiet about him and the light was gentle in his square of window.

Most of his past gunfighting exploits were under-recorded and unreported mainly because they most often were simply that – gunfights. Duels of honor fought out according to a universal set of rules which were so meticulously observed that the law simply never had reason to pursue him whenever some loser crashed to his death under his flaming Colt 45s.

He'd never been tense before a shootout and this day was no different as he moved through the lengthening afternoon shadows out upon the Jubilee Plains. Of course he was fully aware this might prove the most significant day of his life – after he'd killed his rival and won back the woman he loved. Yet his pulsebeat was metronome regular to his touch and when he lifted a tailormade to his lips his hand was steady as the Rock of Gibraltar.

He thought of her as he drew deep. It had been wonderful when they had been true lovers, agony ever since it ended. For how could a man surrender something more important to him than life? It could not be done.

He went motionless at the faint sound of steps on the stairs, relaxed again when he heard familiar voices, Emil Branco's habitual cursing.

He flicked cigarette ash off his tailored lapel and admired his reflection in a window pane, and thought confidently.

Winner Quentin; loser Cardinal. Rip up your tab tickets or come collect your winnings, gents! The end result was as good as set in stone now – wasn't it?

It had been wonderful back in Dodge City where he'd seemingly carried all before him – until that final week. But now, as always, it was only the final score that counted. No way would he step aside for that high-stepping badgeman to claim her love again, leaving him with only the empty years ahead.

Steps sounded along the corridor.

'Go to hell!' the gunman called through his open door.

'Hey, it's only me, Ash.'

'You too, fat man.'

But the footsteps grew closer until the sweating bulk of Branco in one of his vast white pouter pigeon shirts and gaudy armbands filled the doorway.

The man's eyes widened when he saw the immaculate figure seated calmly in the chair by the window. He'd only ever seen Quentin looking like an advertisement for men's expensive apparel in a magazine, but for some reason had expected to find him looking at least a little jittery and ragged round the edges today.

Instead the fellow appeared even more relaxed and impressive than he'd ever seen him – like a man on top of his world. But how could that be, all things considered?

Then the fat man realized he should be pleased to find the gunslinger appearing so calm and reasonable. Plainly this augured all the better for his own purposes.

He rested fists on hips and talked straight.

'Son, I'm in deep trouble—'

'So . . . who gives a rat's?' Quentin cut him off. His tone was easy but his mood had never been stranger. 'What about me, fat man? Whatever troubles you have are nothing alongside mine. I'm just sitting here dwelling on the fact that there's not one lousy soul on this stinking planet gives a damn if I live or die. Well, can you top that?'

This was all Swahili to Emil Branco. If Quentin was looking for sympathy, he must be loco. Who'd feel sorry for any man with his kind of reputation, looks and style? Not a fat and greedy go-getter with too much on his mind – that was for sure!

'Quentin . . . I mean, Ash. I know when I hired you it was just as a dealer. But I'm no fool. The moment I saw you I knew right off that you were one hell of a lot more than just that. What I'm saying is, I've always known you were exactly the breed of *hombre* I might call upon to help me out if ever I was really in deep trouble. Are you following me, son? You seem kind of distracted.'

Ashton had twisted in his chair to stare at the window with a frown. 'What is all that hollering from the street?'

Branco hadn't heard. Now he did. Someone was shouting up to him. He went quickly to the window and drew back the drapes. His cellarman was standing clear of the awning twenty feet below, looking up.

'What?'

'They've arrested Sy, boss. Cardinal beat up on him and jugged him just half an hour ago. You hear what I'm sayin'?'

But Branco had swung away to stare down upon the seated Ashton again, his flaccid face pipeclay white.

'See . . . that tinstar son of a bitch is going all the way!' he croaked. 'I knew this day was coming the minute he closed me down. Cardinal's been after

151

me for six months, now he's pulling out all the stops to finish me off. All right – how much, Quentin?'

'What?'

'How much to gun that iron-jawed marshal? Come on, everybody knows you're a top shootist, maybe even the fraggin' best. So I'm offering you the biggest payday you'll likely ever see to take on what you do best. This is a gun job. No! Not just a gun job – *the* gun job. Are you paying attention . . . and why in hell are you grinning? Did I say something funny?'

Quentin rose and moved about the room with the grace of a boxer. He was smiling but there as no hint of humor in his eyes.

Nervously, Branco watched the gambler circle the room until he halted before him. That vaguely amused expression was gone now, replaced by something harder and colder.

'You're right of course, fat man. Everyone knows I'm nothing but a bad-ass guntipper.' He propped and snapped. 'How much?'

'W-what?'

'To kill the marshal, of course.'

Pure joy flooded Branco's features. 'You guessed? Well, wouldn't take all that much figuring, I guess. Why . . . why I'd go high as five hundred to get rid of—'

'One thousand,' Quentin said, striding to his bureau. 'Write me out a bank check for a grand and get out.'

'Mebbe cash would be safer?'

'Do it or the deal's off.'

Hastily, Branco produced checkbook and pen and scrawled out the check. Wordlessly he passed it over. No words. Branco went to the door, paused to glance back. Ashton was holding a fancy coat up to the light. 'What are you doing, son?'

'Dressing for the occasion, of course. Now get out.'

The fat man's party vanished and Quentin shrugged out of his jacket then set about checking his sixguns as he stood by the window. He was smiling but it appeared more like a triumphant grimace. When setting out for Storytown to kill the man who stood between him and the woman he loved, he'd never expected to be paid for it.

Gene Cardinal stepped from the jailhouse into the deepening afternoon shadows slanting across the street. Ashton stood a hundred yards west with his back to the lowering sun. The gambler was tall and impressive in his elegant wardrobe. But Cardinal wore a brass badge and would not have traded it for any suit of gold.

'Don't do this, boss. You don't have to, you know.'

Ignoring Slow Joe's plea, he set off down into the street. Of course he had to do it. Quentin had issued a direct challenge and he could either take it up or run.

He paused momentarily to study the silent crowd and they in turn saw his face was empty of all expression. He even glimpsed some tears and signs of anxiety here and there as though some were counting him dead already. They knew he was fast, but Quentin carried some kind of lethal aura. Had Joe Wilkes from the Pioneer Saloon been running a book on the outcome, he suspected the heavy money might well have been on his adversary.

He paused on glimpsing Rebecca's marble white face in the crowd. She called his name but he walked on. In his mind, this was not about her, but rather about law and order. And in this man's town, he was law and order.

He halted thirty yards from the man whose shouted challenge had jolted the whole street alert just one short minute earlier.

'This is a mistake, Quentin. This won't solve anything.'

'It will solve your lifespan, Cardinal.' Quentin held up a slip of paper. 'Citizen Branco is paying one thousand so he can dance on your grave. Imagine that.'

'So, this is about money?'

Ashton ripped the check in half and let the pieces flutter to the ground.

'Neither of us believe that, Cardinal! It's all about her, and we both know it. She is mine and I mean to have her again. Forever!'

'You're a fool!'

'And you're dead. Draw!'

They came clear together and it was a dramatic thing to see. But when the fearful roar of gunfire erupted it instantly turned bloody and ugly with first Cardinal then Ashton tumbling in the

154

gunsmoke clouds, crimson showing, their roaring guns abruptly giving way to a sudden ominous silence.

But as the smoke began to clear it was the marshal who was now up on one knee clutching a bloodied arm while his adversary remained on his back with his white face turned to the sky and the startled afternoon birds, as the ghoulish crowd pushed forwards.

'Back up!'

Cardinal's voice rang like a gunshot, as full of authority as ever.

They halted as he limped towards the figure in the dust, and saw that Ashton was not dead yet, although crimson was spreading across his deep chest in a swift dark stain.

Cardinal went down on one knee at the man's side. He folded his Stetson and placed it under his head.

'Why, Ashton? It didn't have to come to this.'

'Sure it did, lawman. I . . . I couldn't have her . . . couldn't let you have her. . . .'

He reached up with great effort and clutched Cardinal's shirtfront.

'You see, it was different for you and me. She threw you out and you took it like a man, never looking back. With me it was different. For thirty years I felt I was some breed of a freak because no woman ever meant a plug damn to me. Then I met her . . . and fell crazy in love. Suddenly I felt as normal as the next man, understood what every-one else knew but me until . . . until that d—'

He coughed and blood trickled.

'Take it easy,' said Cardinal.

'Too late for that.' Quentin's head tilted back and his face was the color of old pipeclay as he stared at up the sky. 'Then she ended it. . . .' His voice was weakening. 'Only I couldn't. But I couldn't leave go, neither. No way. So I tried to win her back . . . she already had her eye out for the next sucker.' He grimaced. 'Hell, I even threatened I'd kill her . . . but I knew I never could. . . .' He grimaced, a half smile. 'But I knew I could kill you and make her come back—'

He broke off, coughing.

Cardinal stared at him. 'Did she believe you?'

'I made her believe it. She was running scared. But I'll tell you she's got guts. I woke up one morning to find that she'd sold out and taken the train here so you'd protect her.'

Cardinal's stare was locked on the white face. 'Me protect her. . . ? Are you telling me she hoped that would happen?'

Quentin forced a grin, no small effort for a man rushing towards death.

'Hey . . . beautiful Becky is no man's fool, lawman. She knew I'd follow her, knew you and I must come to it. . . .' The gambler's eyes widened. 'And glory be . . . she got just what she wanted – again! Can you . . . beat that? Brought me down here just so you could blow me away. And we both fell for it!'

Gene nodded slowly as though in acknowledgment of a half-suspicion now proven.

'You've got it all wrong,' he said. 'Rebecca told me you were the only man she ever loved, that she only left you because she was always scared of really falling in love. That was why she ran. . . .'

Quentin's eyes were wide. 'She . . . is what you just said true, Cardinal. . . ? She really loves me?'

'Gospel.'

A wondering smile creased the gunfighter's face then froze. His head lolled to one side and he was dead.

He'd never seen her looking more beautiful or animated as she circled the office with that familiar lithe stride. Even her eyes, usually so lovely yet guarded, today seemed alive with excitement.

She halted before his swivel chair.

'Gene, are you listening to what I'm saying? Honestly, I've never seen you more serious. But why, in God's name? Don't you see? It's all over and you and I are free to start afresh. I half expected to be dead myself by now . . . we might both have been dead—'

'I don't believe Quentin would have killed you, Rebecca. He was in love with you.'

'I'm not interested in Quentin. He is not—'

'He told me you realized you'd chosen the wrong man to flirt with when you dumped him and he turned ugly,' Cardinal said tonelessly. 'So you panicked and decided to come here . . . knowing he'd follow you and wagering that sooner or later he and I would have to come to it? Isn't that the way it played, Rebecca?'

For a moment she was speechless, the animation fading from her face. That animation which both Cardinal and Slow Joe Pierce, now leaning in the doorway, had found so startling and, under the grim circumstances, so offensive.

It was early the following morning with her former lover but twelve hours dead, yet Rebecca was dressed in vivid colors, enhanced by jewelery and pearls, hair and make-up immaculate and lovely eyes shining – everything about her appearance and manner so starkly at odds with the somber mood which gripped the town following its day of chaos.

This was Rebecca triumphant, and Cardinal was both repelled by it yet at the same time relieved. For he realized he'd carried a secret torch for her ever since Dodge, but now that torch was finally extinguished – forever.

'Gene, what are you saying. . . ?'

He rose and picked up his hat from the desk.

'You told me you loved me, then finished it the moment you'd had enough, Rebecca. As you had the perfect right to do. Then you did the same with Quentin. Only thing, you picked the wrong man that time. He just couldn't fall for someone then accept the kiss-off. He was crazy about you, so crazy in fact that he scared the hell out of you and—'

'Gene, no, I—'

'Let me finish,' he said coldly. 'When you realized you'd played your game with the wrong man, you shifted down here knowing full well he'd follow. All you had to do here was convince him you were still in love with me, knowing he and I would have to come to it. Well, congratulations. It worked just like you planned. Quentin's gone, you're dancing on the man's grave – and I've got a town to see to.'

'Gene!' she cried, but the marshal was already gone.

The lights in the show-up room were dimmed with the exception of the one directly above Slow Joe Pierce's desk, that pool of yellow light under which all lawbreakers both large and small found themselves eventually exposed.

Tonight had witnessed the appearance of the biggest fish of all when Emil Branco had been arraigned for a trial on a date to be fixed on crimes ranging from corruption to coercion, from extortion to fraud and incitement to kill – this last grave charge supported by the testimony of the recovered check made out to the late Ash Quentin.

The last shuffling figure had passed on either to freedom or to the cells below, yet the deputy still sat in place, listening to steps approaching from the gloom beyond the lights until the tall figure of Gene Cardinal appeared before him.

'All right, what crime are you charged with?' he demanded, playing it poker-faced.

'Placing rye whiskey ahead of both love and money,' Cardinal declared solemnly.

'How do you plead?'

'Guilty, with extenuating circumstances.'

'What might they be?'

'I didn't know when to ease up before.'

Slow Joe rose almost swiftly, for him. 'But you do now?'

'I do, your honor.'

'All right, I sentence you to two beers and four whiskies to be consumed right away in the presence of a supervisory officer, namely myself.'

Their eyes locked and they smiled for the first time, hands clasping as youthful deputies watched from the shadows. Then they grabbed their hats and went down the steps into the street with a clatter of boot-heels.

They halted on coming face to face with Harry Slater as he slid from his lathered horse at the hitchrail.

'Howdy, pard,' the rancher panted, nodding to Slow Joe. 'Er, came in to congratulate you on everything, Gene . . . hope you never got busted up or anything in all the hooraw—'

'What brings you in, Harry?' Cardinal asked.

The cattleman turned his hat in his hands. 'Well, to tell you the truth, it's kinda about Muriel, Gene. . . .'

'Thought it might be.' Cardinal threw an arm about his friend's shoulders as Slow Joe muffled a grin. 'Come on, we'll have one at the Indian Queen and you can tell me all about it.'